THE KEY CHRONICLES

The Key Chronicles

Bronze

Addison Holli Sparace

Addison Holli Sparace

To mom:

Who told me she couldn't afford my reading habit.

CHAPTER 1

I never thought that I'd be dumpster diving. Maybe I took my luck for granted, but now I keep trying to stay away from everyone. Ever since my mother disappeared people have been looking for me, telling me to come with them so I can be safe. They want me at an orphanage or foster home. They say she's dead, but I know better. My name is Ariel Wends.

I was rummaging through a McDonalds dumpster, hoping for maybe a nice, hot, french-fry. All I got was a raccoon who used my hand to jump out of the dumpster, ripped my camouflage pants, and then chased me down the street. My long brown hair was trailing behind me, and my gray sweatshirt was covered in muck. I found it interesting that no one paid me any attention, as I ran down the sidewalk with a not so happy racoon chasing me. Eventually I got away and sat in an alleyway with my stomach growling. The world around me was spinning. I needed to *rest.*

I was breathing heavily but once I managed to calm my breathing, I closed my eyes and fell asleep. I had a dream which was different. Normally I sleep in silence and don't dream of anything.

Not this time. I was running down a street with a man chasing me. I thought I had seen him before but couldn't think of where from. He had a gray sweater-vest , tan khakis and black dress shoes, along with his slick brown hair and icy blue eyes. He had a gray stubble that looked very itchy. He looked familiar, but in my disoriented dream state I couldn't figure out why. He was yelling something I couldn't quite make out. It kind of sounded like he was yelling, "I can help you. I know your mother's alive. I could help."

I came to a halt. So did the man who was following me. I was looking for my words, but I couldn't find them. At last, I said, "No Shilo, I don't want your help." Then I ran off. This time the man named Shilo didn't follow me.

The next vision in the dream was more terrifying. I was standing by a pile of rubble, a man, a terrifying man in front of me. Half of his face, scar tissue. The other half just scarred. His greasy black hair was slicked down on his scalp. His black suit paired perfectly with his steel gray eyes. He looked at me with a toothy look, revealing yellow teeth. He pushed me into a hole in the ground.

Then I woke up, gasping for breath and the cold autumn air stung my hazel eyes.

Shilo, Shilo. I know I have heard that name before. Where from though? Then it hit

me like a rock in the head. Shilo, Uncle Shilo, yes that's who the man must have been. If I remember right, he had a gray stubble and chocolate brown hair just like that man.

Also, anytime I saw him he had on a gray sweater-vest, tan khakis and black dress shoes. Did he live in that outfit? Sure, it seemed so. I ignored the other dream though, it creeped me out too much.

But I was still left with other questions. I wanted to know why I was having a dream about Shilo? I hadn't seen him in at least a month. We weren't even that close. I heaved a sigh and slowly, I crept out of the alley to find it was dark outside. No one was there. I looked down either side of the street to make sure nobody saw me. I booked it towards the Harlem library. See what I did there? I BOOKED it to the library. See I can be funny. Now back to what I was saying.

I ran to the library, ducking behind parked cars when anyone walked by. Weird. Why were there people out at night? Now you might be thinking Ariel, why would you be going to a library? The answer to that is I have no idea. I just thought, well no one will be there tonight. Was I terribly wrong? Looks like it wasn't night like I thought. It was early morning around 7:00 am and guess what? Just because I'm so lucky, that is the time the library opens.

That got me thinking, how long had I really been sleeping? I think it was mid-afternoon when I fell asleep. That dream went by so fast it only felt like a few minutes. But then I did spend some time pondering the dream. Honestly, nothing made sense. I was hoping I could climb a tree and stay up there for the night like I do sometimes. But because the library was open, there were people milling around in the parking lot and underneath the tree I usually climbed. I pulled the hood of my sweatshirt over my head so no one could see my face or my hair. People just passed me, paying me no attention. As much as I wanted to go into the library, where they for sure had warmth from the autumn air - I never did. I was too nervous someone would notice me.

To be fair, I was the girl whose face was on the news. I didn't look at people and they didn't look at me. I went around the back of the building and found a ladder leading up to the roof. I climbed for what felt like forever. When I finally reached the top, nobody else was up there. Thankfully it was a flat roof with a slight lip so I could see over the edge, but no one could see me.

When I first got to the roof, I thought it was nice! One step up from a tree. I peered over the edge of the roof. It was a 2-story library so I could see a small portion of the city. I sat for a while and contemplated my dream and what it meant. Nothing really came to me. After a while, my stomach started complaining that I needed to eat.

I climbed down and yet again went searching for food. Except this time, I didn't go looking in a dumpster. Instead, I went to a local soup kitchen at 252 W 116th street. After 5 minutes of walking, I arrived at the soup kitchen. I immediately wished I could have those 5 minutes back and could go somewhere else. Right there sitting at the table closest to the counter was my uncle

Shilo, wearing his signature gray sweater-vest with his tan khakis and black dress shoes. Seriously he could have passed as an elderly man if he had not had his shiny brown hair and icy blue eyes that were dancing with life and a mischievous gleam.

Of course, he spotted me right away and made a gesture with his hand that meant come here.

"Long time no see Ariel" he said. His tone was cold, but it had the slight sound of concern and sympathy.

"What are you doing here?" I said through a forced smile and gritted teeth.

"Now that's no way to greet your uncle, now, is it? Come sit down, we have a lot to talk about."

"What is there to talk about?" I said hastily. A tone of rage was creeping into my voice "You know where she is don't you? "I asked.

"Know where who is?" he said.

I knew very well he was just playing with my mind. Shilo was trying to confuse me, but I wouldn't fall for it.

"You know who I am talking about. Don't play dumb, Shilo. And just in case you have lost a brain cell, I am talking about my mother."

"Ah, Salma. She was a good sister. Too bad. Oh, I know where she is, but the real question is how you are going to find her and get to her in time." Before I could ask more questions, he got up and walked away. I did not dare to follow. I sat in silence for a bit and ate a Devil's Food doughnut. Those are my favorite, but it still tasted like dust. I couldn't help wondering why Shilo had found me today, the day after the dream.

After a while, I walked out of the soup kitchen, and I walked down the street. Oh, did I make a mistake. It was now 8:15 a.m. and the streets had hundreds of people including police officers, who were going all different directions. I, being the walking mess I was, forgot to put my hood up and was noticed almost as soon as I stepped outside. I was noticed by an officer wearing a sort-of formal blue shirt with black pants and a black bullet proof vest with white words inscribed with the initials *NYPD*.

He approached me and said, "Hey kid your name is Ariel, right?" Every part of me told me to lie! They will take you away! Don't do it! But I knew that it was no use. If I lie now, I knew it would just hurt me more later. So, I gave in. I gave a grim nod and said, "Yes sir, I am in fact Ariel Wends."

"I see," the officer replied.

He muttered something into the walkie-talkie I couldn't quite make out. "I'll have to ask you to come with me." I took one last look around and then I asked, "What orphanage or foster care am I going to? "

The officer looked at his pad of paper and said, "You will be going to Mr. Downs foster care, just 10 minutes west of here." I took a deep sigh and looked at the library. I couldn't bring myself to look at the officer, so still looking away from him I said, "I understand, I see there in no use running so I will come with you."

The officer replied with, "You are right there is no use running."

Then I sat down in the front seat of the police cruiser, and we drove off, except this time I'd accepted defeat.

CHAPTER 2

As we were driving, the only thing I could think of were my uncle's words, "Oh I

know where she is but the real question is how are you going to find her and get to her in time?"

What did that mean? Why couldn't life be fairer? Perhaps, I don't know, maybe let me live a normal life. With a normal uncle. Most of all with my mom there. You might be thinking what about your dad? Don't you wish he were here? To be honest I have never met him. My mother said that he died. She never went into details. She said they were close, but I could hear a bit of resentment in her voice. I knew better than to ask questions. But I knew was his name was Frank.

When we arrived at Mr. Down's orphanage, we stepped out of the car and walked up to the front gate. It was a chain-link gate. It wasn't that tall, but it was tall enough where you couldn't climb it. The gate opened and we walked inside.

The first thing I noticed was how happy the atmosphere was. And I hated it. Going to a place I didn't want to go to was bad enough, the last thing I wanted to be was happy.

The interior was fancy for an orphanage. It had shiny oak floors, off-white walls, and a grand staircase with red velvet carpeting. It had a few plants scattered around, a white marble fireplace with a crackling fire inside, 3 light gray couches with a red and gold rug. It smelled of old wood polish and jasmine. There was a man wearing a black suit with a white shirt and a cherry red tie. On his face, were a pair of black glasses. His feet were interesting because he was wearing Star Wars ankle socks with Chewbacca and Han Solo. He also had on brown formal shoes. He had short gray hair and a small beard and mustache. His eyes were a light brown, and his smile was warm. Still, I really didn't want to be there.

"Hello Ariel, my name is Calon Downs, and I run this orphanage."

I forced a smile. "Hello, Mr. Downs! Pleased to meet you."

"No, please call me Mr. Calon Or Mr. C, whichever you prefer."

"Alright, Mr. Calon that's okay with me."

"Okay, then the other kids are upstairs in the bedroom. It is the 3rd room on the right. Please introduce yourself and I will be right up. I have to talk to this officer first."

"Right."

I ran up the right staircase and down the hall. Then I turned back in the direction I came. I was used to people talking behind my back but this time I wanted to know what it was about. So, I listened in.

"Calon, you know her mother is alive, why hide it from her? You know that if she finds out..."

"Officer, trust me. You know Frank is most likely to be alive too. They just need some time. I know they will be alright."

I'd heard enough and I wanted to jump out and say, "HAHAHAHA I already knew my mother was alive but not my father! ' But I had to restrain myself, so I walked back to the room to meet the other children. There were 3. The oldest was fourteen, the same age as me. One of the boys was thirteen and younger than me by half a year. The girl was thirteen and older than the youngest boy by a few months. The 14-year-old introduced himself first. He had pure blond hair, pale skin, and his cheeks were a little pink. He wore a cyan shirt with bleached jeans. He had a little scar on the back of his right hand.

"Hello, I'm Ben Cruise."

To my surprise, his voice sounded quite formal.

"Hello Ben, I am Ariel Wends. Nice to meet you!"

We shook hands and I introduced myself to the next kid. The girl. She had red hair with tan skin and red freckles on her face and arms. Her eyes were light green. Her lips were light pink and she either wore a lot of blush or she was naturally flushed. She wore a pink sweatshirt with a white cat on it. She had on black leggings.

"Hello!" her voice was bubbly and happy "I'm Ginger Sparrow, it's nice to have another girl around. It gets boring here."

"Pleased to meet you, Ginger. I am Ariel Wends "

We shook hands and I moved on. The last kid had dark brown skin, and curly black hair that looked like it wanted to be an afro but wasn't quite there yet. His eyes were seafoam green, and his hands were light pink and a little calloused. He wore a blue and white striped tee-shirt with denim blue jeans.

"Hi, um, my name is uh - sorry I get nervous around people I do not know - my name is Jerry Miller" he sounded nervous like I might hurt him if he said something wrong. Otherwise, he sounded happy and content.

"Nice to meet you, Jerry, I am Ariel Wends" I reached out to shake his hand. I could see he didn't want to, but he did anyway. Then Mr. C came up. I couldn't read his expression, but he looked weary.

"Hello, children. I assume that Ariel here has introduced herself?" Everyone gave a slow nod. "Ben, can you give her a tour please."

Ben looked around the room. He looked at Jerry and then he looked at Ginger. He stared at the floor for a minute before saying, "I guess "

He took my wrist and led me out of the room.

He brought me down the hall and past Mr. Calon's room.

He broke the silence by stopping at the left side of the long hallway. He said, "How did you get here?"

I really did not want to talk about it, but I thought it would be rude if I didn't, so I answered him.

"1 week ago," I started, "when I fell asleep there was a big, loud, crash. It sounded like a glass vase shattering." I couldn't look at Ben, so I looked at the floor instead.

"The first thing I did was run into my mom's room. We were really close so if anything happened, I'd always go see her first, but she was gone. Her windows were still closed. Her bed was semi-made and..." I choked up.

"You don't have to continue," Ben said but he looked like he wanted to do more to help me. But if that was the case he'd need to know more.

It's ok, I will. Just give me a second. I counted to ten then continued. As we stood in the hall, I kept talking. "That was the night that neighbors called the police. That was also the night that I had to flee my house and hide in alleyways because they wanted to take me here." I gestured around the hall with my hands. "That's my story."

"I am so sorry Ariel."

"You can feel anything for me but don't feel sorry", I snapped "I know she is alive. I heard them talking. Never mind, just keep on with the tour. We have been standing in this hall for 5 minutes."

He led me down the hall into a large room. On the far wall, there was a large oak fireplace with a huge mantle. In the middle of the room was a big birch farm-house style table with 10 chairs around it. The walls were the same off-white as downstairs. The floors were dark oak hardwood. In the center of the table was a vase with roses. In front of each of the chairs was a placemat with a knife, a spoon, a fork, followed by a plate and bowl. There was a roaring fire in the fireplace. On the mantle were some tiny succulents and a picture frame with a picture of all the kids at the orphanage.

"Dinner hall," Ben said and then he dragged me to the next room. The next room had bookshelves built on the left wall with all sorts of books. There was a small oak table in the corner with 2 chairs. On the table was a box with some paper and drawing supplies like crayons, colored pencils, markers, paints, paintbrushes, and normal pencils. In one corner there were a couple of chairs with a rug.

"This is sort of like an activity's room where we can come anytime to do stuff, read, paint, draw or just talk. "

He led me to the next room. It resembled a classroom with 10 desks and a whiteboard in the front of the room. There was also a teacher's desk. It had a couple of book shelves and a table with 10 laptops.

"This is the schoolroom," Ben explained," We still have school. It is different though because we only have classes on Mondays, Wednesdays, and Thursdays. We have Tuesday and Friday off. Same with the weekend. We have that off too."

Before he could drag me out, I asked Ben, "Why are there 10 seats when there are only three kids?"

"The orphanage can hold up to 10 kids. The others came of age and left, or they got adopted" Ben continued, "I will show you back to the bedrooms."

I never really focused on the bedroom. It had soft gray walls with white floor-length curtains. It had yet again 10 beds, each with a soft oak dresser at the end of it and a soft oak nightstand next to the beds. It had a fluffy gray rug in the middle. In one corner was a pile of stuffed animals and in another, bookshelves with a large choice of books for any age. There were picture books, and chapter books too. The beds were all twin-sized with white pillows and white sheets. They had light gray comforters with pastel yellow stars. Right across the hall was a bathroom. Now that I think about it, it looked more like a kid's bedroom than a fancy building. Then Mr. Calon came into the room and announced, "Ariel please come with me."

CHAPTER 3

Ginger, Ben, and Jerry fixed their eyes on me. I stepped forward, left the room, and followed him downstairs. We passed the marble fireplace and went into the room next to it. He sat down at a desk, and I sat on the other side.

"Ariel, I need to tell you something."

"I already know my mother and father are alive." Calon's warm smile turned grim.

"How could you possibly know that?"

"I knew that from the day of my mother's disappearance that she was still alive, but not my father."

"Ariel I'm sorry for not telling you earlier but-"

"Mr. Calon it is quite alright. I just wish someone could tell me about my father."

"Your father Frank, he was a good man. He had chocolate brown hair, warm brown eyes, and a warming smile. But one day he just disappeared with but a single note that read. *Dear Salma, I will be back soon I swear. If you want to know where I'm going it's to get you the one thing you dreamed of. You will love it.*

Love, Frank Wends."

He pulled a letter out of his pocket that read the exact same thing he'd just told me. I examined the words written in fine cursive. The handwriting was loopy and unfamiliar. It honestly made me a bit uncomfortable, you know. The handwriting of my father I'd never met, never seen. It was right in front of me.

I looked up from the piece of paper. "I need to go now. If I could find them, you don't know how much it would mean to me. "

"I agree." Agreed Calon.

I tried my hardest not to scream EEEK THANK YOU SO MUCH!

"Ok but where do I go first? How do I get there? What do I do when I'm there? Where is "there"?"

"I will answer all your questions. I am going to say something first though. I won't allow you to do this by yourself. You have 3 options 1.) Don't go at all 2.) You bring Ben with you 3.) You bring Ben, Jerry, and Ginger."

"Well not number 1, so I'll choose number 3. We can make this a family adventure since right now they are the closest family I have."

"Alright then, Ariel, we will inform the kids tomorrow."

I made my way up the stairs and walked into the art room. It was Tuesday so I had no school. I sat at one of the tables and got a piece of paper and a pencil. I didn't know what to draw so I tried to draw me and my mom standing outside since she was always gardening or going on walks. I tried to remember her delicate features. I put my pencil on the paper and I drew. I drew a circle for her face and on the bottom of the circle I drew a chin. Then the rest came to me naturally. 30 Minutes later I had a fully shaded picture of my mom in a flannel, jeans, and hiking boots. I stood next to her with her arm around me. We were standing on a hiking trail. Without realizing it, I drew the time we went hiking at Glacier National Park. We went camping and fishing a lot on that trip, I was staring at the picture for a while when I heard a voice from behind me,

"Hi Arie. It's Ginger. Is it ok if I call you Arie for short instead of Ariel?"

I looked up from my drawing and saw Ginger standing above me in her bubble gum pink sweatshirt.

"Sure," I replied and went back to looking at my drawing.

It looked so real, but my thoughts were interrupted by Ginger. Did I really want her to come with me to find my parents? I decided why not. If we need a slightly annoying 13-year-old in a pink cat sweatshirt, Ginger will work perfectly.

"Can I see your drawing?" Ginger asked.

"Sure, why not." I picked up the drawing and handed it to her.

"This is - this is awesome Ariel. Where did you learn to draw like this?" she sounded awestruck.

"My mom taught me. That's who the drawing is of. My mom and I were at Glacier Park that day."

"You're very talented, Ariel! Can you teach me? I love to draw but I'm only good at cartoon drawings, anime and that sort of thing" She set my drawing on a table and walked over to another table. I carefully put the drawing in my pocket. When Ginger returned, she was holding a drawing of an anime girl with short red hair. shorts, and a yellow shirt. I do have to say it looked pretty good. I was only good at realistic drawings.

"I will teach you to draw realistic, on one condition" she looked a little nervous but didn't say anything.

"You teach me to draw in a cartoon-ish style. I don't know how to draw like that we can teach each other."

She gave me a smile that said I get to teach someone to draw and I'm happy. "Deal," she said. Then I started to draw a new person.

"Well, we will have to do that some other time. It's time for dinner," she said.

We walked to the next room and sat down, and we ate grilled cheese sandwiches. When we were done everyone went downstairs, except for me. I sat in front of the large oak fireplace and sat in silence. I thought about the fact that in one or two days I'd be leaving to go to who knows where with 3 kids I really don't know very well. I got up and walked downstairs to go find Mr. C. He was in his office just where I had last seen him. I sat down at his desk, and I asked," can you tell me where I'm going, please "

He took a minute to answer but he finally said," You will be going to Jericho, a suburb outside of New York City. "

"Thanks," I replied. Then I got up and walked away.

I wondered what I would do in Jericho. I walked upstairs and into the bedrooms. I sat on my bed, and it was comfortable. I laid down and stared at the ceiling. It was now 7:30 pm. I decided it wouldn't matter if I went to sleep before the curfew of 8:00, so I went to sleep. I didn't dream of crazy uncles chasing me, so I was relieved. I still had a dream though. I was in my apartment with my mother, and she looked at me and said, "My sweet daughter, we have very little time."

"What do you mean?" I said hastily.

"You will know when the time comes. You will find three keys in three different places. Remember the order of Bronze, Silver, Gold. If you do it any differently, I will be gone. Your father will be gone with me."

"Where are you? Please tell me," I pleaded. There was a tear coming down my cheek.

My mom crumbled to dust and my father stepped forward. He looked just like Mr. Calon had described him. He had chocolate brown hair and warming eyes, though all the warmth seemed to have seeped out of them. His smile had lost the same thing and was cold. When he spoke, he spoke in a raspy tone I knew couldn't possibly be his.

"Your mother, hah a joke" he said

"Sh-shut up" I said" you know you love her, where is your warmth?" I asked." You say this as if you have met me," he replied, "but you haven't."

"Even if I have never met you before I have heard good things, and this doesn't match what I have heard."

His image flashed showing him with all his warmth. His smile and his eyes didn't feel so cold anymore. He looked at me and said, "Good if you can see through that you will do just fine" his voice seemed cool and calm now.

Before he had any time to ask questions he turned to dust. I felt the pressure in my ears pop, and I got a splitting headache. My eyes shot open with my heart beating so fast it threatened to break my rib cage. It was 7:00 a.m. according to the wall clock. Everyone normally got up at 8:00, so I had some time to process my dream. Was God trying to tell me something, or was I just going crazy? I had opted that God was trying to tell me something because I didn't like the idea of going insane.

Ok then there was that key thing. What was the order gold, bronze, silver? No, no was it silver, bronze, gold. Nope that still seemed wrong. What about bronze, silver, gold? Yes! That seemed to be it. I thought of it in that order for a few minutes then moved on.

Next my father. One minute he was this cold harsh, weirdo person saying he thought my mom was a joke. Then next minute he's this semi-caring father telling me I will do just fine.

I was going to get up and walk around but then I heard footsteps down the hall. Everyone in here was asleep so I figured it was Mr. Calon. I closed my eyes to pretend I was asleep. He opened the door and stood in the middle of the room. He had a glass cup in his right hand and a spoon in his left. He hit the spoon against the cup and yelled," Rise and shine everybody!"

I slowly got up just to be a bit more realistic. I stifled a yawn and stood and stretched, like Ben, Jerry, and Ginger

"Why a bit early today?" asked Jerry. He sounded a little annoyed.

"Well, you see everyone you don't have school today, and yes I know it is Wednesday."

Ginger came to the front "Oooooh why don't we have school?"

"Well, you see Ariel must tell you something "

Ginger, Jerry, and Ben fixed their eyes on me. I stepped to where Mr. C was standing.

"I um..." I gulped, "How would you feel if I told you we are all leaving to go to some

town with a weird name to try and find a key?" Nobody answered me.

"Well, everybody, we are going on a field trip (do orphanages even have those?) to a nice little town named Jericho to do who knows what. When I say everybody, I just mean the four of us."

I pointed at them. I got some weird stares. It was awkward.

"She is right. She has to do a series of tasks in order to find her parents and she asked to bring all of you because she says she hopes to become close as a family." Ben looked at the ceiling.

"So, your telling me tha-"

"Less talking and more packing" Mr. C chided.

Everyone put some clothes in a bag and got dressed. Mr. C Left the room and said, "Have a nice trip!" Leaving me with 3 very confused teenagers to explain everything to.

CHAPTER 4

"Are we going on a field trip?" Ginger asked.

Talking over her Jerry said, "Does it involve heights? I am allergic to heights."

"It's less of a field trip to answer Ginger's question. I guess you could say it's more of an adventure. And I don't know it there will be any heights." I left out the details about him being allergic to heights.

"So pretty much we have to find 3 keys and the bronze one is supposed to be in Jericho. Or we are supposed to find someone or something there that can help. This is to...."

I sighed. What if I told them it was to benefit me? Would they still want to help? "It's to find my parents. I'm sure that once we find them, they will let you stay with us if you want to." Even though I'd said that they could stay I didn't quite know if my parents would agree.

No one answered but finally Ben stepped forward.

"Of course, we will help, and it's just not to be able to live at your house, but because we are friends now."

"Right, guys?"

He turned and faced his friends.

"Of course, we will help!" Jerry and Ginger said in unison. I didn't hear any bitterness. They sounded genuine.

"You guys are the best!" I said.

"I know," Ginger replied.

"Follow me. Bring everything you want in those burlap bags." I said "And before anyone

asks, no I don't know where we're going."

I smirked but no one saw. Mr. C was at the bottom of the stairs by the door. I heard him mutter something under his breath. I couldn't quite hear what.

"Ahh children" he sounded a bit sad but continued, "you are all very unique and I have looked after you all while you have been here."

"I'm unique huh" Jerry murmured. Mr. C ignored him.

"I will miss you all, but you must prevail." he took a pause then he said, "Ariel could you please come with me?" Surprisingly he sounded a bit upset.

"Yeah, yeah sure" I turned to my friends "I'll be right back."

Then I followed him into the office. He stood behind his desk and put his hands on his desk. He looked more pale than usual, and more tense.

"Why didn't you tell me about the keys?" He said in a low tone.

"I didn't know before. And I'm not sure."

Mr. C got up and slowly walked around the room. "Ariel, you don't understand what you've just gotten yourself into."

I tensed and I got a cold chill. "What do you mean?"

"Those keys...They are the keys of earth. Taynam.

"He killed my wife. He is a very bad man."

"Who exactly is Taynam and what does he have to do with keys?" I asked.

"He is a murderer, thief, trickster, and liar. He could scam a beggar out of his last coin. If he is holding your parents' hostage..." He paused and his breathing became shallow.

"No, no, no way. This is too dangerous," he said.

"How exactly?" I pleaded.

"Listen to me Ariel. If you must take on the burden of doing this, you should know that if you encounter Taynam or his followers do not listen to any promises they make, OK? They will deceive you. They want the keys to unlock the earth core."

To me this didn't make sense. "What's an earth core?" I asked.

He looked a little stunned that I didn't already know what it was.

"The earth core is a thick obsidian circle - shaped column that is in the middle of the earth. It holds 3 keyholes: a bronze keyhole, a sliver keyhole, and a golden keyhole. When the matching keys are returned and the keys of earth are reunited with their respective keyholes, the person that put them there will be able to bend water, fire, and earth to their will. This makes them the most powerful person on the planet. Taynam, as I said, is power hungry. He wants to create a new world. That would mean destroying this one. It appears he has taken your parents hostage because he knows you are the one that can get the keys and they are the keys needed to open the bonds he is using to hold your parents captive. He will keep them alive because he needs the keys to open the core."

"And how do you know this?" I demanded.

"Because..." He hesitated. "Because I used to work with him."

That hit me hard. Finally, I found an adult that won't leave then BAM! I found out he used to work with the person who wants to literally make the world explode. That's just great.

"Wait – so, wait. You used to work with the ever so evil Taynam who wanted to make the world go bye-bye?"

"When you put it that way it sounds like I wanted to help him do that. But to be fair I didn't really want to do it. In a way I was forced into it. I needed money, and he could provide it, in a way, huh." I muttered, "So, then how'd he kill your wife?"

"That's a touchy subject" He said, "but I guess I owe you some explanations."

"You're bloody right you do." I said.

"Like I said, I worked for him. I was in a way his personal guard. I guess you could

say he wasn't that nice. He'd say some hurtful things. On October 15, 1998, I told him that I wanted to resign from my job, that I didn't want to work for him anymore.

He said that it was perfectly fine. I gave him my badge and walked out with my wife. I knew something was up. he'd never just let me walk out. The next morning, when I woke, instead of finding my wife, there was a letter next to me. It read, *so you don't want to work for me, eh? You won't pay for that, your wife will.* I never saw her again so I'm not quite sure if she's dead, but she had lung cancer, so I'd assume she is no longer with us." He looked at the ceiling.

"Wait, that was five years ago? It's 2003."

"Years don't matter," he said.

I didn't reply.

"I am going to tell this to everyone - whether you want me to or not."

He looked like he wanted to protest but he didn't.

I walked out of the room, no goodbyes or anything.

I relayed the story to my friends the best way possible - telling them someone wanted to blow up the world. Aren't I so nice! Nobody said anything for a while.

"Well, let's get going", I said as enthusiastically as I could for someone who'd just been

told that the world might be exploding.

We went to the nearest bus stop and caught a bus. When we boarded, the person I least wanted to see was sitting there. Shilo Wends was sitting in the last seat. I wanted to jump out of the window and run. We made it about two miles out of the city when he made his way down the aisle. I ran to the front of the bus and asked the driver to stop.

"But it's not a city. It's just a road with forest and thick brush on the sides.", the bus driver said.

"It's ok!" I said.

He stopped the bus.

"Come on guys," I yelled down the aisle.

Shilo started walking a bit more briskly. We ran out the bus doors just as they were closing. Shilo was at the front, but the bus was already gone. We were on the side of the road with just three burlap sacks. Ben put his blanket under a tree and wrote in his journal.

"What was that about?" Jerry complained.

"Shilo, my uncle. But he's like this weird creepy dude." I said.

"It looks like we are camping here tonight," Ben said, looking at me as if saying "Thanks a lot. Now we were stuck in a forest by the road."

"I'm going to go walk in the forest" I said.

Forests always made me feel better. Their animals and wildlife made me feel at home. Even though I was a city girl I went camping a lot.

I walked about a half mile. I was going to go another half mile when I heard an ear – piercing scream coming from the same direction as camp. I did the first thing that came to mind, I ran back to camp to make sure my friends were ok.

CHAPTER 5

They weren't ok. When I got there, I stopped at the edge of the forest. Jerry was hovering over Ben who was laying on the ground scratched and bloodied, but still conscious. Ginger, where was Ginger? I looked around the campsite and spotted her. She was pinned up against a tree with this...thing standing a foot away. I had no idea what it was; it looked like something straight out of a horror movie. I'd never seen one, but I had an idea of what it was. One of Taynam's minions.

It was now right up on Ginger. From the waist up it had on a black leather jacket, with a white shirt. Its hands were dry and leathery, it had four fingers with sharp claws, its hands webbed with bulging purple veins. The monster's skin was a pale orange, like it had been coated with Cheetos dust. The head was shaped like a snake with bright Emerald green eyes, the lips were thin and looked like they were covered in tissue paper. On his head was a mop of greasy black hair. But from the waist down it was almost worse. It had scaly legs that looked like they could belong to a dragon, (if dragons were real, and based on what I was seeing, I wouldn't be surprised if they were).

The scales were black with splashes of silver scales here and there. Its feet were like its hands, papery and leathery. You could see every purple vein and it had four toes, each equipped with its own set of razor-sharp claws. I didn't know what to do so the first thing I did was throw a rock at it. It looked mildly annoyed but un-pinned Ginger who looked like she hadn't been harmed, though she looked a bit disgusted. It waddled towards me. I didn't know how I was supposed to get rid of it or chase it away, so I tried to use what information Calon had told me about Taynam.

First, it was either not in a hurry to get to me, or it was slow. I hoped it was slow. When it got within smelling distance I was sure that it had burned every one of my nose hairs. The thing smelled like rotten fish that had taken a bath in a dumpster that had not been emptied in a month.

My eyes watered. I didn't want to talk but I did. "Y-you work f-for Taynam, don't you" I gagged. You could almost taste the monster's stench.

"Master is Taynam," the monster bellowed. Its voice was musty and dry like he hadn't

talked in a year.

"Uh-huh, I see. Taynam and I go way back," I lied. "He would be livid if you killed me."

"No proof. Prove to me you are not lying," said the monster mockingly, as if he knew I'd have nothing.

"Taynam had a guard named Calon Downs, right?" I asked.

"Yes," said the monster suspiciously.

My confidence grew. I said, "And he didn't want to work with my friend any longer, correct?"

"True," said the creature.

"Yes, yes of course it's true. I - I helped Lord Taynam with that. He sent me to uh... extract his wife."

I might have said something wrong, but the creature replied with, "But you are merely a

girl."

"I was 9 then and it was an easy job. Calon was a heavy sleeper," I argued. The monster looked at me.

"I judge you worthy. I will let master know you're here."

"NO," I yelped. The monster looked at me confused. "I mean no it's alright, he uh sent me here to infiltrate this group of kids."

"Very well!" said the dragon - snake thing. Then he poofed into a very toxic smelling cloud of smoke.

First, I ran over to Ginger who'd looked good and had recovered. All she had was some dirt on her sweatshirt.

"Are you ok?" I asked.

"Yeah, I'm ok. But you, you were awesome!" she squeaked. "Telling him you knew who he was, Brilliant! "

"Thank you, Ginger! But we should go see if the boys are ok."

We walked over to Jerry who was still standing over Ben. I got down on my knees and kneeled next to him.

"Are you alright, Ben?" I asked him.

"Yeah, I'm fine," he said. I asked Ginger to stay there and asked Jerry to follow me.

"How'd he get a gash on his arm?" I asked.

"When that thing came it went for Ginger, I'm not sure why maybe because she's wearing hot pink, but Ben put himself between that thing and Ginger. The monster swatted him aside and left him with that gash."

"He's such a dummy, he's lucky I have gauze and antibacterial medicine." I said "Could you and Ginger go get some wood please, for a fire. We will need to go to Jericho tomorrow."

"Sure," he said rather glumly.

"Thanks!" I said. I gave him a hug just so he'd not be so sad. It worked because he looked back like his normal self. He and Ginger walked into the woods. I got my medical sack and kneeled next to Ben.

"Don't try to save Ginger again, you dummy. The monster would have killed her and you if it had wanted to, ok?"

"Yes ma'am," he said rather amused.

"Now give me your arm so I can bandage it," I said.

I helped him sit up and lean against a tree. I took his arm, but it was feverishly warm.

"Shoot," I said under my breath. It was infected already. Ben didn't hear me, which was good.

"This is going to hurt" I warned.

I put on some of the anti-inflammatory which made Ben yelp. I wrapped the gauze around the wound by the top of his shoulder. I helped him up and he sat down on a log by the fire pit, which was lacking a fire.

"Stay right here," I said and went to pack up all my stuff that was on the ground.

When I came back Jerry and Ginger were starting a fire in the pit. We sat around the firepit and ate Beef Jerky and drank bottled water. It was almost dark, so I told everyone I was going to sleep. I grabbed my blanket out of my bag and put it under a tree and drifted off. I didn't go into a dream but, I unwillingly kept recalling the words that Mr. C told me about how he used to work with Taynam. In the morning we packed up camp and started our mile walk to Jericho, Long Island. We walked in silence, which meant more time for me to sort out my thoughts. I kept remembering the exact words of Mr. C. I felt bad for him. Poor guy only had orphaned kids as close family and now we are on an adventure to find the 3 keys and my parents, and we have a high chance we might die. We finally got to Jericho and let me tell you it is an impressive city.

We walked around the park for a bit. I'd brought a bit of money I'd had from when I'd lived with my mom. $20. We went to Jericho Commons and went to the store. I bought some rations. Stuff like more Beef Jerky and M&Ms (M&Ms aren't rations but I wanted them, ok?). We left and walked on the streets and just looked around. We had no idea what to look for in order to get this first key, but we had to try, I had to try. That's when I spotted him. A teenage kid, maybe 16. He had dark brown hair, pale skin, gray eyes, black tee-shirt, jeans, and white sneakers. But the most interesting thing about him was the fact he had an iron sword strapped to his side. I pointed at him.

"Over there, guys," I said. We walked over to the boy.

"Um excuse me, may I ask why you have a sword strapped to your side?"

"Ahhhh, you must be a chosen one or you wouldn't see my sword," replied the boy. "One must always be prepared for a Drython attack, weird ugly snake - dragon guys."

"What do you mean we are chosen ones?" I asked.

"You are one of the 8 people chosen in 10 years to try to kill Taynam, correct? I am Sam." He said. "You want the keys right, to unlock your parents."

"Correct. But how'd you know about my mom?" I asked.

"The same thing happened to me. I just wasn't successful in saving them," Sam replied, regret filling his voice.

"Sorry," I said. "I'm Ariel. This is Ginger. This is Ben, and this is Jerry."

"Nice to meet you", Sam said. "Now you might want to know where the bronze key is and I'll help, but first I'm going to give you this dagger, Ariel." he said.

He handed me a dagger with a golden blade and a black hilt. I hooked the sheath to my belt.

"Thank you but won't people ask about it? "

"Unless they were chosen at birth by God to fight Taynam, then no," he said.

"Also, here's 100 dollars. Go to *Blades for Blades* down the street with this so you can get your friends weapons too."

"Thanks, Sam. Could you tell us about the key again?" I asked.

"Sure, like I said, Taynam killed my mother and father after failing to get the keys and get to them. You must find the key in a cave a little bit farther from here. You have probably 5 days until he decides that you won't end up getting the keys at all and he kills them. The cave will have some scratches around the entrance, from past people that have entered. Make sure you put a mark when you enter as well. You will pass through Plainview and go south."

"Thanks Sam," I said, but he was already gone. We walked to the shop Blades for Blades and the owner almost immediately noticed us as fighters against Taynam and gave us all weapons he'd thought would work - except for me since I had a dagger. Ginger got a beautiful sword - an ivory blade with a golden leather hilt. Ben got a black bow with a silver drawstring and a few quivers of silver arrows. And last Jerry got a dagger with a bronze blade and a tan leather hilt. The kind man insisted it was free, but we still gave him 50 dollars. We rented 2 rooms at a cheap hotel - one for Ginger and I and one for Jerry and Ben. It was midday but while the others walked town

I stayed in my room and thought about the 5-day dead-line. This was going to be interesting.

CHAPTER 6

That night I couldn't sleep. I lay awake in my bed. I knew I needed to sleep, so I made some tea and my eyes turned to lead. I drifted into a dream. First, I was back in New York City in my mom's apartment. That was the night I had tried to get her to talk about dad. She wouldn't ever tell me. She'd just mumble things like, "he was awesome" or "he's a military captain." But I knew he wasn't a Military captain because one of her other lines was, "he works as an accountant in Long Island." We were on the couch, and I kept pushing her to tell me the truth. But she snapped and said she was going to go outside for some air. That night she was outside all night.

Then the dream shifted, and I was again talking to Mr. Calon except I was seeing it from his point of view. I could see all the Horror on my face when he said he worked for the enemy. I could feel all the hurt he felt when I didn't say goodbye. Suddenly my sorrow and guilt multiplied as I felt so bad, I hadn't said goodbye.

I woke up and I still felt all the guilt. I knew I needed to do something about it. I looked at the clock. It was

7:00 am. I looked at the white phone sitting on my night-stand. I picked up the phone and dialed Mr. Downs' Or-phanage, and hoped I wasn't too loud. Ginger was still asleep, and it was an old-time phone so I couldn't exactly get up and move. He picked up the phone.

"Mr. Downs speaking."

"Uh Um hi Mr. C. This is Ariel..." I couldn't see his face, but I could hear his voice soften just a touch.

"Oh, hi Ariel are you alright? Why'd you call is every-one alright, Ben, Jerry, Ginger they're fine rig-"

"I'M SORRY," I blurted out. There was a long silence. "I-I'm sorry I was upset with you and that I... I didn't say bye. I'm sorry for all of it. And yes, everyone's ok."

"Ariel, it's ok, if I was you, I would have been upset too."

"We are heading to Plainview; in case you want to know." I told him.

"Ok, just be careful."

"We will," I said, then the phone went silent. I sat on the edge of my bed and heaved a big sigh. Why did I feel closer to my friends and Mr. C than my own parents? I didn't know but I didn't think that was good.

I got up off my bed and went out into the hallway of the hotel. I took the elevator to the bottom floor and went out into the lobby. The interior was impressive. It had beautiful gray wood flooring. The front desk was dark oak with a white marble countertop. Right across from the front desk was a living room area that was set around a white double sided marble fireplace, like the desk. It had two dark gray armchairs

On the other side were 2 more dark gray armchairs. Down the hall from that was a room with around 30 pine tables each with a set of 4 ash wood chairs. In the middle of the room was a bright white three-tier fountain. All the tables were surrounding it.

On the back wall was another counter of Mahogany. It had glass boxes of food on it. Eggs, bread, bagels, sausages, bacon, and waffle batter. There were fruits like apples, bananas, grapes, and strawberries. And more dry foods like small individual boxes of cereal. On another counter on the right of it there was a soft drink dispenser, water, and milk in a mini fridge along with different kinds of yogurt, next to a small box of blueberry muffins. There were also plastic, forks, knives, and spoons. With glass plates. The counter on the left hand 3 toasters, 2 waffle makers to make waffles, butter, and a small basket of fruit. The whole hotel smelled like cleaning supplies and citrus.

In the lobby sitting in one of the chairs was Ben. I was surprised to see him down in the lobby. He seemed tired last night. I walked over to him. And tapped him on the shoulder. He turned and faced me.

"You should never walk into a room and tap someone on the shoulder without talking first," he scolded" I almost punched you in the face."

I gave him a smile "Yes sir," I said jokingly.

"You, ok?" he asked.

"Yea I'm fine, but what about you? It's normal for me to wake up early, but not you."

"I'm ok," he said. I wanted to believe him, but I could hear the tension in his voice.

"Spill it," I said, straight forward.

"Spill what," he said, he sounded a bit surprised I knew something was up.

"Ok Ben, tell me what's wrong I might be able to help," I pleaded.

Ben paused.

"Fine," he said. "But you keep this between you and me, fair enough?"

"Fair enough," I said, but I didn't think I even knew the meaning of fair anymore. My life wasn't fair. But nobody was. He stood up and faced me, looking at the bandage on his arm where the creature had gotten him.

"I used to be the oldest and so normally I'd have to show strength or whatever, but now that you're here I feel like I have a huge weight off my shoulders. Like I don't have to be the only person they have. It made me feel relieved and that......that left time for my own thoughts. I'm scared, Ariel. I'm scared of traveling around the world to fight some guy I didn't even know existed until a while ago, I'm scared I'm going to die. I'm scared I'm going to lose you" he said, now on the edge of tears.

"Me?" I quietly whispered; I could feel my face go red.

"Jerry and Ginger are awesome friends," he said. "But they were always younger, and they always hung out together seeing me as their older brother. Leaving me alone.

Now I finally have somebody the same age to talk with, to see as my friend." He finished up with a tear coming down his cheek.

"Ben, I'll always be your friend but never your little sister!" I said jokingly and gave him a hug. He gave a small smile and loosened his tense shoulders and sunk into my hug. I rested my head on his shoulder.

"I'll always be your friend." I whispered so quietly that I thought I said it in my head.

"I'm glad," he said, pulling away from my hug. He heaved a sigh. "We'd better go wake up Jerry and Ginger."

"Yeah, I guess," I said.

I walked to the elevator, Ben behind me. I stood in the quiet and waited for the 4th floor to come. We got off and I went right, he went left. When I got back into our hotel room I went over to Ginger's bed. I shook ginger.

"Wake up!" I said into her ear. She groaned and pulled the pillow over her ears and disappeared into the blankets. Lucky for me I knew the keyword to get Ginger to listen to me. she had told me when I'd met her.

"Oh, suit yourself, I was just off to go get some pancakes," I said, slightly louder than the rest. She poked her head out of the blanket so only her face was showing. She cocked her head slightly like a curious puppy.

"Pancakes?" she whispered as if the word was poison.

"Pancakes," I agreed.

"PANCAKES!" She yelled excitedly and jumped out of bed.

Her hair was a rat's nest of tangles and knots. Her light blue tank top was crinkled and her matching blue shorts, with stars, were riding up. So occasionally she'd pull them down.

"Sorry Ginger, no pancakes."

"No pancakes?" she asked sadly, like a kid you told you couldn't go to Disney world. But "I did get you up!" I said happily.

She made weird noises. "Ugh I should have not told you about that word. You will NOT speak of this, ok?"

"Yup ok," I replied.

She went off to the bathroom to change. When she came out, she was dressed in her pink sweatshirt and denim ripped jeans. Her hair was done up in a bun. She looked beautiful. My face reddened when I realized I'd still been in my black tank top and sweatpants when I'd talked to Ben.

"You look really pretty," I said quickly to Ginger and ran into the bathroom to change.

I put on my Camouflage shirt and a pair of ripped jeans. I washed my hair in the sink, dried it, then brushed it. I put it up in a high ponytail and slipped on my sweat-shirt. I put on my sneakers and opened the bathroom door, expecting to see Ginger doing Ginger things. Instead, I saw ginger talking to Jerry in one corner and Ben leaning up against the door clutching his arm where he'd been scratched. He quickly took it off when he saw me.

I held up my finger at him to tell him I'd be right there and walked over to Jerry. Jerry and Ginger were having a deep conversation that stopped when I got there.

"Hey Ariel," Jerry said, wearing a little panic. He was dressed in his striped shirt and black jeans. I decided against asking why he looked worried.

"Hi," I replied like I'd never talked to him.

"Just wanted to say good morning," I said.

"Good morning," he said and went back to talking to Ginger.

I headed over to Ben. He was dressed in a white tee-shirt, jeans, and sneakers. His sword at his side.

I had my dagger at my side too, still wondering how other people wouldn't notice.

"Hey," I said awkwardly.

"Hi," he said back. Jerry and Ginger were still talking but didn't want to take any

chances. I quietly opened the door and pulled Ben out into the hallway and closed the door.

"Are you ok, I know earlier in the morning you were a bit nervous." I asked him. Suddenly he became very interested in his shoes.

"I was hoping you'd forget that" he mumbled back.

"How could I? You're my friend, you don't have to be embarrassed about being nervous... or scared. None of it," I said, surprised by my own words. But I knew I meant what I said.

He sat down on the floor and silently cried into his hands. Had I said something wrong?

I made sure the others were still talking, and they were so I sat down next to him. He took his hands off his face and rested his head on my shoulder.

"Did I do something wrong?" I asked quietly.

He gave a sniffle before saying, "No it's just, nobody's ever been nice to me like this. Not even Jerry or Ginger. I -I just feel terrible thinking about." He didn't finish the sentence, but he said, "I think it's time I tell you about my old life."

CHAPTER 7

I perked up. He knew a lot about me, but I knew barely anything about him.

"It started this year. I went to school, and my best friend Everly looked at me and...

and she said I was the worst friend ever. I hadn't done anything wrong; we hadn't had a fight. Nothing," he said, lifting his head up off my shoulder.

He looked around the hall which was still quiet. He took my hand, but I was still too busy listening to really notice.

I tried talking to her the next day, but she just asked me "Who are you?" like we'd never met."

"I don't mean to interrupt but, what school did you go to?"

"I went to a high school in NY City. Townsend Harris."

I nodded my head. He looked down at my hand that he was still holding onto, his grip getting tighter as he got into more depth of his old life.

"I tried talking to some of my other friends, like Connor who I'd talked to the day before. He asked me the same question as Everly. I talked to more people, even teachers and they all asked the same question. I thought it was a prank but there was no way that the teachers would be in on it. I raced home to my mother and father, but no one was home. I waited until 6 pm but they still weren't back. The next morning at 7 am I heard a knock on the door. I rushed over thinking it was my parents, but when I opened it, there was an officer standing there. 'Your parents have been reported missing, possibly dead,' she had said. I turned into a heap on the floor. ' No, they - they can't be they were here yesterday morning ' I'd said. Then she said to take what I wanted, and I was going to Mr. Downs."

Ben started to cry again, and I gave him a big hug.

"Now I understand the new kid that was there must have been working with Taynam - we wiped their memories."

He gripped my hand so hard it hurt, but I let him. Ben was sad, scared, angry, and stressed. I could relate to that.

"I know, I understand. He took my life from me too."

He cried into my shoulder leaving a wet spot. Once he stopped, I helped him get up. He was wobbly like a newborn colt. I took off my sweatshirt and tied it around my waist. I took his hand again and we walked into the room. Jerry and Ginger were waiting on one of the beds with all our items packed. Ginger looked at me and Ben clearly thinking are they ok? But, instead, she jokingly said, "Well this is known," seeing me and Ben holding hands, his grip stronger than ever.

But Jerry saved me from answering. He noticed how red and puffy Ben's eyes were. He rushed over.

"Are you ok?" he asked, scanning his wounds.

"I'm fine," he replied but before Jerry could ask what was wrong, he said, "I'd rather not talk about it."

He looked at me and walked over to the bathroom sink so he could look at his face in a mirror. Jerry followed peppering him with more questions about what happened. Ginger walked over.

"What happened out there? Is he ok? What's up with you holding his hand? You looked a little uncomfortable."

"I can't really say what happened. It's not my information to share as to why we were holding hands, that was because he got emotional and so I let him hold my hand," I said, a little embarrassed.

"It's ok you don't want to share his secrets, but I don't really think that's why he was holding your hand. I think someone has a little crush on Ariel," she teased.

I could feel myself blush.

"Let's drop this conversation," I suggested.

"We will definitely revisit this." She replied. I ignored her and walked into the bathroom where Jerry and Ben were talking. Ben saw me and gave me a look that said help me, because Jerry was still asking him questions.

"Hey guys we still have to get to Plainview; we only have 4 more days," I said.

I could see Ben was grateful we were leaving. We went
down to the lobby and stopped at a cafe for breakfast. I
got a coffee, since I had a restless night Jerry and Ginger
got orange juice and Ben got nothing. I guess our talk ru-
ined his appetite. We caught a bus to Plainview, and I was
pleased to see that my uncle was not there. We sat on
the bus for a good half hour. There were only a few other
people on the bus. A girl with black hair and glasses was
reading. A mother and her son were in the front. We were
the only people in the back. Even though Ben assured
me he was fine, he still seemed like he had more to say
to me. He looked at the girl with the black hair. The bus
driver wasn't looking so I quickly switched my seat, so
I was sitting next to him. He didn't even notice until I
tapped him on the shoulder. He gave a quiet gasp.

"What did I tell you about sneaking up on me like
that?" he said.

"Sorry," I mumbled.

"Hey, don't be so serious I'm just joking around." He
gave me a light, joking punch on the shoulder.

" I know; you just looked worried." I pointed at the girl
with the black hair. "That's

Everly, isn't it?" I asked.

His eyes looked sad. I almost regretted asking about
her when he said, "You know me too well already. Yeah,
it's Everly."

The bus stopped and she got off at another bus stop.

"Don't think about it and you will be fine," I said re-assuringly. 15 minutes later we were getting off the bus ourselves. We were in Plainview.

"So where do we go from here? "Jerry asked.

I took a map from the box by the bus station. We all huddled around it. I pointed to a spot on the map." Sam said we were supposed to go-" I was interrupted by a girl.

"You guys fighting Taynam?" she asked casually.

"Uhhhhhhh" I wasn't sure how to answer that question. "Yes?" I said with a squeak in my voice.

"Ah ha! Knew it! I'm Brooke," she said.

Brooke was beautiful. She looked around 15 with platinum blonde hair that was done up with a braid on each side. Her skin was pale with a little bit of pink on her cheek. Her eyes were cobalt blue. Her features were soft. She had on a white blouse and light blue jeans. She had a silver dagger sheathed in a black Draython skin sheath. Her voice was soft, and she smelled like cinnamon and nutmeg.

"Hi, Brooke. I'm Ariel. These are my friends Ben, Ginger, and Jerry." They gave an awkward wave.

"Nice to meet y'all."

"Nice to meet you too," Ben said to all of us.

"So, how'd you know we were fighting Taynam?" Ginger asked curiously.

"Well because I can see your weapons you know. Normal people don't carry around weapons, plus I'm a fighter of Taynam, or at least I was. I didn't know what to do when my dad was taken. Then I went to Mr. Downs. You went there too, right?" she asked. I found it slightly unsettling that she knew we had gone there.

"Um yes, yes, we did go there. How'd you know?" Jerry asked, already slightly paranoid.

She gave out a small laugh like it was a silly question. Then she looked at him and saw he had meant it.

"Oh, I guess he didn't explain it," she said. "You know you're a fighter of Taynam when your guardian goes missing. It could be your grandparents, mom or dad, aunt or uncle, older brother or sister. Anyone who looks after you. Then, depending on where you live, you'll be taken to a special orphanage where you will be told how everything works. In the New York city area, it is Mr. Downs who would be helping you. I went there so I knew you did too," she explained.

"That makes sense," I said. "Sort of." She looked at me with her calm blue eyes.

"Do you want me to show you around the town, not a lot to see but it's home."

"Sure", I asked, looking at my friends. They nodded in agreement.

She took my wrist and dragged me down the street to an outdoor buffet. I hadn't even realized it was lunch time yet. We sat down at one of the tables and one of the waiters came over.

"Would you like to order anything?" he asked.

"I'll get a ham sandwich with American cheese," I told him, and he wrote it down on his pad of paper. He turned to Brooke.

"I'll get a crispy chicken salad with honey mustard dressing," she said. He etched it down "Thank you." He smiled and turned to Ben.

He looked at his menu. I could see he wasn't hungry, but he knew he should eat

something.

"I will get maple bacon doughnut." The waiter wrote it down and turned to Jerry.

"I'll have a spicy BLT wrap," he said.

He turned to Ginger.

"I'll have the same thing," she told him.

"I'll be right back," he said and walked into the restaurant. Almost as quick as he went in, he returned with a pitcher of ice water. He set it down on the table along with five glasses.

"Your food will be done in 20 minutes," he informed them.

"Thanks," we said as he walked away.

"So, I was thinking that after this I could take you guys to a few of my favorite places where I go when I'm bored," Brooke said.

We nodded in agreement, and she squealed. She sat there and talked about what we could do. I wanted to look at the map to see where we would have to go, but I didn't want to be rude, so I excused myself and went to the bathroom. I set it down on the marble counter and studied it carefully. We entered from the north so we would have to go south. Ginger came into the bathroom.

"Are you ok? You have been here for 5 minutes which isn't normal for you," she asked.

"Yeah, just wanted to look at this without being rude," I explained while holding up the map.

"OK," she said and led me back out. We ate our food, paid and left.

"My favorite thing is coming up!" she said with enthusiasm. She led us over a hill and to a little shack. It was labeled "Bikes for rent."

Brooke handed the man 50 dollars and we all picked out a bike. Mine was white with black faded streaks. She took us up over another hill to a dirt road. After Ben's forest incident I wasn't as comfortable in the woods. There was a hill we went down that helped us pick up speed. We raced the path with Brooke in the lead. She told us to stop. Instead of going the way the path told us to go, we veered off to the side. She took us through twisting trees until we reached a little clearing. It had some sort of white fog around it. She stepped forward through it. But we couldn't. When we didn't come through. She came back with a sheepish smile.

"Sorry, I forgot I need to grant you permission." She placed her hand on our temples and the white fog cleared revealing a small clearing.

In the middle of it there was a koi fishpond. On the east side there was a tent big enough it could comfortably fit 8 people. On the west side there was a small

wooden room labeled "shower." The south side had a
fire pit with log benches. We entered the north end. The
whole area was covered in flowers and wildlife. It smelled
like fresh air and honey. There was a small garden full of
veggies nestled neatly in a small area by the fire pit. The
place was breathtaking.

She skipped out to the pond and said, "This is home!"

"Why couldn't we get through the white fog?" Ben
asked her.

"I covered it in an invisibility spell so you can't get in
without permission," she explained holding up a book titled "*Beginners' guide to illusion magic.*"

He nodded his head clearly thinking the same thing
as me, great on top of this crazy situation we can also
learn magic?

She pointed to the sky which was streaked with pink,
yellow, and orange.

"It's getting late, we'd better sleep. You can stay in my
tent if you want; or you can sleep outside. Whichever.
There's a shower room too if you need that."

I took a shower and piled my hair up into a bun. I took
out my sleeping bag and set it up by one of her flower
gardens. I took out one of my personal items I didn't tell
anyone I brought. A stuffed cat with a light pink bow. It
was my first stuffed animal, and I couldn't sleep without it. I stuffed it back in my bag and drifted off into a
dreamless sleep.

CHAPTER 8

"Hello? Earth to Ariel?" Ginger said, hovering over me. I opened my eyes and yawned.

"Ugh you're so easy to wake up. I was hoping I'd have to pour ice water on you or something," Ginger said, sounding rather sad.

I smiled at her. "You wish," I told her. She let out a laugh and walked away.

I got up out of my sleeping bag and headed over to the campfire. It was early in the morning. Maybe 7:00 am. Everyone was still in their pajamas. We all sat by the campfire and warmed ourselves up. Everyone slept outside besides Brooke and Ginger who had a little sleepover, I could hear them talking and laughing all night.

Brooke had out a cast iron skillet and was frying eggs and bacon and breakfast sausages. She handed each of us a hand-crafted wooden plate piled with bacon, fried eggs, and sausage links. The food was hot and tasted just like home. We picked up our forks and ate.

"So, how'd everyone sleep?" Brooke asked everyone. Me, Jerry, and Ginger all answered, "Good."

But Ben mumbled, "I didn't sleep," then realized everyone heard him and said, "Good."

"Well today I was thinking I could teach you guys some illusion magic! "Brooke said, sounding really excited.

Ginger's eyes widened to four times their original size. A crazy smile crossed her lips." "You mean it?" Ginger asked quietly.

Brooke nodded.

Ginger let out a tiny squeak. "YAY!" She shouted.

Brooke smiled and said, "We should all get dressed first."

I walked up to the bathroom and got changed there. I hopped in the shower then I got

dressed in my jeans and sweatshirt. I combed my hair which was now down to my waist. I walked outside. Everyone stared at me.

"What?" I was a little nervous.

"You look beautiful," they all said.

"Thank you," I said and felt my face go red. Ben stared at my eyes.

"Since when do you have purple eyes?" he asked me.

"I don't have purple eyes," I insisted.

He stared at my eyes longer.

"Now they are silver," he told me.

I ran back to the bathroom and looked in the mirror. Sure enough they were silver. I blinked twice and panicked when they were still silver. And still staring into my reflection they turned dark brown.

I walked back outside, and people were still staring at me.

Brooke walked up to me. "I think you're kaleidoscopic," she told me.

"What's that?" I asked her.

"It means that your eyes change color depending on your mood. It's rare and is only found amongst fighters of Taynam. It can be a bit of a weakness because your enemy can tell your feelings. Your friends can too. It will be harder to lie about feelings. The good thing about it though is fighters of Taynam who are kaleidoscopic are guaranteed to learn illusion magic," she said.

"That's cool, I guess. What are the emotions my eyes correspond to?" I asked.

"Hazel: Happy / neutral. Violet: nervous.

Green: scared.

Cobalt blue: sad.

Amber: embarrassed.

Silver: confused.

Dark brown: panicked.

Storm gray: angry.

There could be more but I'm not sure. Those are the known ones."

Brooke reached into her pocket and pulled something out.

"Here I think you should have this." She handed me a small compact mirror the size of a cookie. It was dark purple. "I thought you'd want it so you could check your eye color. I had a friend who was kaleidoscopic, and he always carried one around in case he needed to see his eye color."

"Thank you," I said and gave her a hug.

She nodded. Everyone else was so quiet I forgot they were there. I turned and faced them. Ginger, who tended to get too excited with these kinds of things came running at me and gave me a big hug.

"That is soooo awesome. I wish I was a kaleidoscope. You're so lucky! You can learn magic easier than I can! You're so lucky," Ginger said, Jerry came over and plucked Ginger off me.

"It's really cool," he said, dragging Ginger away before she could reattach herself to me.

My eyes returned to hazel. It was weird like I could feel when they changed colors. Then Ben came over and gave me an awkward hug. My eyes turned violet.

"It's really cool that your eyes can do that. It's even cooler that you can learn illusion magic." His voice drifted off as he noticed my eye color.

"Do I make you nervous?" he asked with a smirk.

Like Brooke said there wasn't any use lying considering my eyes would give it away.

I looked down at my feet. "No," I mumbled.

He was clearly unconvinced, but he dropped the conversation.

"So, what triggered it? My eyes? Because they most certainly weren't like this before. All color changey and stuff."

Brooke thought about that for a minute. "Well, I'm not a hundred percent sure. Maybe it triggers at a certain age, or something dramatic or exciting happened. But I'm just guessing that fate decided it was time."

Well, that wasn't a good explanation, but I let it slide. As Brooke explained to the others, they could only learn certain spells like invisibility or doubling, I was lost in thought of what triggered my eye color changing. I could only really hear half of what she was saying.

"Doubling is a spell that lets you create two of something. Whether it be yourself or a book. There will always be the original and a fake. The fake is like a hologram and can't be picked up or touched. To double something, close your eyes and think of one

thing. Imagine that thing being split in half so there are two of it. Then think of pushing it out of your head" Brooke explained.

We copied her instructions. Jerry and I were the only ones who got it on their first try. The second time Ben and Ginger got it.

"Good now, remember that. Invisibility is easy. Imagine yourself or an object

surrounded by white fog. Nobody can see through the fog, but they can touch it. Imagine pushing it out of your head forcing it to become a reality," she explained

We all got it on our first try. She was right, it was easy. To return to normal she told us to imagine the fog going away. Then we were visible.

"Those are the only spells I can teach you three," she pointed to Jerry, Ben, and Ginger.

"But you Ariel, I can teach you a few different spells. "

She taught me how to move things with my mind, how to make something look like something it's not, she also taught me to talk to and befriend animals, then summon them to my side.

We were about to go get lunch when I yelled, "WE FORGOT."

They all looked at me like I was crazy. Then Ben realized what I was saying.

"She's right! We are supposed to be heading to that cave today!" Ben looked down at his feet when realization hit Ginger and Jerry.

"I'm sorry Brooke, we might not see you again, but we have to go! Thank you so much for your help. "

"Whoa, Whoa, I know it's not my business but where are you guys going? "

I explained our mission to go south to save my family, how we must find the keys. I explained it in vivid details. I finished with, "And now we are down to 3 days."

Brooke looked stunned.

"You have to let me come with you," she pleaded. "After all, I did help you and everything and I think you owe me a favor." She argued.

"But Broo-"

"But Brooke nothing," she snapped" I'm coming with you "

I looked at my friends and we came to a silent, silent agreement. Brooke was coming and that was that. There was no convincing her to stay here, where it was safe. We rode our rental bikes back and returned them. We walked on the south road leading out of town.

"The cave has a bunch of scratches from the past people who have entered" I told them" All five of us will need to leave a mark; apparently it's a tradition. Be on the lookout."

We walked for 2 miles. My feet were getting tired and still no sign of the cave. When I thought I couldn't be more tired, we broke into a sprint because it started to pour down rain. As we were looking for a place to get out of the rain, I spotted a cave tucked snugly in between two trees. The cave had over a hundred marks on the outside. This was it. The hard beginning to a hard reality. Nothing would be the same again. I grabbed a stone off the ground and we each left a scratch on the outside of the cave.

We stepped inside the cave and Ben started to say something like, "this is it", when he clasped his arm and hit the cave floor. Jerry and Ginger went to start a fire for warmth, and I sat down next to him and eased him into a sitting position. I took his hand off his arm and unwrapped the bandage. I had forgotten it was infected. The gash on his arm was a charcoal black and the surrounding area was glowing a fluorescent green. I called Brooke over and she sat down next to him.

"What gave him this gash?" she asked

"The same thing your dagger sheath is made of." I told her, "A Draython." She shook her head and pulled something out of her backpack.

"This should help," she said handing me a bright red balm labeled "Drayton poison remover."

"Why me?" I asked. "I don't know how to use it," I said.

"Just spread it on, then wipe it off. And for why you should do it, he trusts you the most," she said with a smirk.

That got a snicker from Ginger and Jerry. I shot them a warning glance and they quieted down. The others sat down by the fire they'd made ignoring me and Ben. My eyes turned dark brown. I panicked, what if it didn't work. I spread the red balm across the wound and left it there for a second and wiped it off as Brooke told me.

When I wiped it off the fluorescent green was gone and was replaced by his normal skin color just slightly paler. The black in the gash was gone, in fact the gash was gone, and it was just a thin scar. He opened his eyes and I slapped him on this good arm.

"Ouch what was that for?" he complained.

"That's for not telling me that your arm was infected and bothering you," I said, and my eyes turned an angry shade of storm gray.

"You're... mad at me?" he asked.

"Of course, I am. You didn't tell me your arm was infected! If Brooke hadn't given me this balm you could have died," I said, my eyes turned cobalt blue.

"I didn't want to worry you," he said quietly.

"Nice to see you care about me, Cruise, but you worry me more when you don't tell me things," I scolded.

A small smile creeped onto his lips. "Nice to see you care about me too, Wends," he said.

"I care about everyone here," I mumbled. He tried to stand up.

"Uh-uh you stay down there. "

"Fine," Ben complained. "But in a half hour I'm getting up. Whether you like it or not." I didn't argue. I brought him over ONE of my M&Ms.

He looked down at his hand. "Only one?" he asked. I dumped a few more in his hand and he was satisfied.

Half an hour later we were packed and ready to head deeper into the cavern.

"This place is creepy," Jerry complained, stepping over cobwebs.

"I agree," I said.

"Me too" Ginger said. Ben agreed.

Brooke didn't say anything.

I walked over to her. "You, OK?"

"Yeah, let's just say I've been here before."

CHAPTER 9

"Have you been here before?" I asked.

"Yup I'm a Vetcher to remember?" Brooke responded.

"I have no idea what a vet rear is." I told her

"Not a vet rear, a *vetcher*. That's the Dutch word for Fighter. Taynam - when he was human was Dutch so fighters of his are called Vetchers."

"I get it," I told her.

"I have been here before. I remember when I was little, I'd have nightmares about it. Then one day my father went missing. When I went to live with Mr. C, he told me about this scary world within a world." She shuddered.

We walked in silence until a bend came around to a forked road. Down the road on the left you could hear running water and the other was dark and quiet.

"I say we try the darker path first. Scary is normally the right way," I said. Nobody said a thing.

We walked down the path finding a dead end. I tried using Allusion magic to get through the wall thinking it was a magic barrier. No matter how hard I used my mental strength I couldn't push through the wall.

"Looks like it's the other path, this one is just a dead end. No magic," I informed them.

We walked back down to the fork and started down the other path, the road where we could hear the running water. We walked for a while with the sound of water getting louder. And then it opened into a huge cavern. We ducked behind some trees to get a good look at the place without being seen by anything or anyone that may be waiting for visitors.

The ceiling was 30 feet above. There was a waterfall running down the far back of the wall that ran into a stream that carried it out of the cavern through a small hole, just big enough for a mouse.

There were large pine trees and weeping willows. I saw small clusters of flowers sprinkled here and there. Right next to the waterfall there was a doorway, that's where we had to go. It looked easy, too easy. The cavern was by far the most beautiful thing that I've ever seen, but it still had an eerie feel to it. Like something was watching.

Waiting. Listening.

"Everyone, stay quiet... I don't think we are alone," I warned.

"Okay" they whispered.

I peered around the edge of a tree we were hiding behind. I didn't see anything. I signed with my hand for them to follow me. We stepped into the middle of the clearing. All I could hear was the rushing waterfall and my friends' faint footsteps behind me. We started walking briskly to the exit when I heard a loud grunt. I looked at my friends."

"Was that one of you?" I squeaked.

They all shook their heads no.

"It was me," a deep voice called. I quickly glanced around the room. Nobody was there.

It was like all the shadows in the room were speaking to *me.*

"Looks like somebody needs the key to find their poor parents," the voice teased.

I felt someone tap me on the shoulder, but all my friends were standing in front of me, speechless and just as scared as I was.

All the shadows in the cavern drifted into the center of the clearing. A swirling cloud of shadows and dust formed. The outline of a tall man formed. He was partially see-through. He looked like he was all black smoke.

A 7-foot-tall person made of black smoke.

My eyes changed to a very bright green. He could tell I was scared. "Ahhh, I see. It looks like we have a kaleidoscopic," he said.

"Wh-who are you?" I managed to say. I am shaking badly now. My eyes turned an even brighter lime green.

"I guess I could tell you since you're not going to live long enough to tell anyone," he scoffed.

His figure turned solid.

From the waist up it had on a black leather jacket, with a white shirt. Its hands were dry and leathery, it had four fingers with sharp claws; its hands webbed with bulging purple veins. The monster's skin was a pale orange, like it had been coated with Cheetos dust. The head was shaped like a snake with bright emerald green eyes, the lips were thin and looked like they were covered in tissue paper. On his head was a mop of greasy black hair.

But from the waist down it was almost worse. It had scaly legs that looked like they could belong to a dragon. The scales were black with splotches of silver scales here and there. Its feet were like its hands, papery and leathery. You could see every purple vein and it had four toes, each equipped with its own set of razor-sharp claws.

It was the same monster that almost killed Ben.

He must have seen me gawking. My eyes turned a very violent shade of stormy gray. I was no longer scared. I was full of rage.

"Miss me?" he asked.

"What do you want, don't you know we are working with you?" I asked sweetly.

"I'm not as stupid as you think, Ariel. I let you get away knowing we would face each other again someday."

My sweet smile melted away into what it really was. Rage mixed with fear. My bottom

lip quivered at the sight of the scaly creature.

But my eyes stayed stormy gray mixed with a light green.

My hand drifted to the hilt of my dagger. My friends' hands drifted to their weapons and

Ben unslung his bow.

The monster wasn't fazed that we'd taken out our weapons.

"So, are we going to get to the fighting part?" Brooke asked. She seemed calm as ever.

"If that's what you wish." He extended his claws and took a swipe at Ginger.

She jumped to the side and his poisoned claws missed her.

We ran around the cavern playing a very dangerous game of tag. Ben took an arrow out of his quiver.

He put it in his bow and fired. It pierced the monster's skin. He growled looking more annoyed than hurt. He yanked it out of his hand which was oozing liquid silver.

Blood of the monsters.

The wound quickly sealed over leaving his hand with just a white spot.

I kicked him in the chest, sending him to the ground. I held my dagger up and pierced his hand and he let out a howl. I was about to pierce his chest when he appeared behind me and pushed me to the ground. His foot on my back made me wheeze. I struggled until my leg was free and kicked him in the tailbone. He lifted his foot and I rolled out of the way. Brooke tackled him, sending him stumbling forward. I kicked him in the stomach, and he wheezed.

For a moment it looked like we were winning but then everything went wrong. He started thrashing like an angry bull sending Brooke flying backward. He completely ignored me, Jerry, Ginger, and Ben thrashing and hacking at his feet. He stopped in front of Brooke who had her dagger at the ready. He swatted her dagger, sending it a few feet away from her. Right out of her reach. I focused all my mental energy on helping Brooke. I tried the doubling spell on Brooke, trying to make two of her for a distraction. But it was too late, he struck Brooke across the stomach with his poisoned claws.

CHAPTER 10

"No!" I screamed at the top of my lungs.

Tears poured down my face. I could feel all the anger swelling up inside me.

All the anger from when my mom was kidnapped, the anger from when I'd been lied to. All the anger I felt for Ben when he explained his past. All the anger from every time I'd been hurt.

It boiled inside me. Then it all spilled out. I charged the monster turning invisible coming up behind him. I smacked his jaw, shattering it in the process. He let out a shriek and when he turned to claw me, I divided my conscience into four separate parts.

Then before my eyes 3 of me bubbled into existence.

Four of me surrounded the monster plus my friends. Shouting insults and stabbing with our weapons we brought him to his knees.

"Any last words?" Ben asked, raising his bow.

"This. Is. Not. Over." The monster wheezed.

"I think it is," Ben said, letting his arrow go. It pierced him in the chest and his body turned limp on the floor.

Just to satisfy my thought I stabbed his lifeless body with my dagger. I rushed over to

Brooke who was laying on the floor.

Her breathing was shallow and the four-claw mark gash on her stomach was turning a nauseated color of bright green. The four scratch marks were black as could be.

"No, no, no, no," I said, sitting next to her. She gave me a weak smile.

"Hey, Ariel," she whispered

"Are you ok? No that's a stupid question. What balms or potions do you have I can use to heal you?" I asked, frantically searching through her bag.

"There's nothing you can do," she said weakly. She coughed a terrible rattly cough.

"No! You have to have something," I said with a tear rolling down my cheek. The others came over with tears spilling down their faces.

"Yeah, what about the stuff you gave me, it was the same creature." Ben said, you could hear the pain in his voice.

"Yours was a light scratch. A warning. Mine was an angry, full-fledged attack. The gash is deep, my regret deeper," she said. She looked so calm, so at peace it made me hurt.

"I have done so many things I wish I hadn't," she said. A single tear fell off her chin and onto the ground.

"For instance, one of those regrets was wishing I had spent more time with *you.*" she said, letting out another rattly cough.

We took her hands. "No, you can't leave me like this - you can't leave us like this," I

said, and ruffled her hair.

"I just have a few requests before my time is up," she said. I looked down at her gut. It was turning the rest of her into that nauseated color of bright green. She saw that I was staring at it.

"It doesn't hurt," she promised me, "Just like a really tickly feeling," she said.

"Okay..." I said quietly, finally coming to terms with the fact she couldn't be helped.

"My requests are first, when I... pass, turn me into a flower, plant it at Mr. Down's. For a memory. Second, take care of your friends as well as you took care of me. Third, take care of my secret, cover for me... and lastly tell Calon that I said hello." Tears dribbled down her cheeks.

"I promise I will," I whispered. I hugged her close.

"I'll miss you guys," she said to all of us.

When I couldn't answer, Jerry did.

"We'll miss you too," he said, his face turning red. She sucked in a deep breath.

"Bye," she wheezed.

Her chest rose and fell. It didn't rise again.

I cried, my tears pouring down my cheeks like everybody else in the room. Then I remembered my promise.

Pulling myself together as much as I could I focused on a memory of us. She was showing me her favorite flower. A poppy.

I focused on that thought and poured my thoughts into her body. She transformed into a poppy. I scooped up the flower and placed it in an empty bottle. I took Ben's hand on my right and Gingers on my left. Jerry grabbed onto Ginger.

I looked up at the ceiling and whispered, "Brooke says hello."

CHAPTER 11

As much as I didn't want to, I pulled myself up off the ground.

"Let's keep going," I said through gritted teeth.

I wasn't going to wait around for someone, or something, else to claim my friends' lives. I let go of their hands and walked over to the doorway, my eyes filled with grief. I peeked around the door to make sure nothing was there and signaled with my hand for them to follow. Nobody said a word. After a couple of minutes, I decided to break the silence.

"Is....everyone alright?" I asked. I knew it was a stupid question, but I didn't know what else to say.

"No," Ginger said, her voice muffled with tears.

"Definitely not," Jerry said quietly.

Ben didn't say anything. I felt terrible, he'd already lost so much. His parents, his best friend, and now his second-best friend. Nobody could endure that much trauma and not feel bad.

I took the lead, planning on talking to Ben about it later.

"I know that we are in a rough spot, but for now let's focus on the good things," I tried. "What good things are there to focus on? Ben almost lost his arm, we are lost in a cave with no way out, and Brooke's dead," Jerry said.

"Focus on the good things like… unicorns and rainbows." That got a small laugh out of my friends.

"Make you a deal, if we can figure out how to get out of here with the key, we can be sad later," I told them.

I waited until they nodded. We started up a conversation that involved a lot of laughing. And I tried my hardest to keep it that way because that's how Brooke would have wanted it. And now I wouldn't be able to look at a poppy flower without being sad. We walked for what felt like forever when we came to a small doorway. And I mean *small.* We had to crawl to fit through the doorway, it was only 3 feet tall. We all got down on our hands and knees to crawl through, which was more difficult for Ben who was still trying to keep weight off his arm.

We emerged in a room. It was small. The walls were dark gray stone bricks. The floor was plain concrete. The room was damp and musty. It smelled like dust and humid, thick, air.

Jerry gagged. "I think this place is bad for my nose hairs," he gagged.

"Agreed," the others jumped in.

There were no windows. No doors. No way out.

In the center of the room stood a golden pillar stand. On top was a bronze key with a glass cover over it.

"This is too easy," I muttered to myself.

"Ariel's right," Jerry agreed.

I looked around the floor. Now that I saw it up close. I could see the panels. There was a rune on each of the tiles.

One tile looked like a snake wrapped around a pole. One tile looked like flames in a circle.

The last tile looked like a crescent moon with three little stars surrounding it.

"It's a puzzle," I told them.

"Of course, it is," Jerry said to himself.

I summoned 3 rocks using Allusion magic.

I threw the first rock at the fire rune. It went up in flames, but the damp air kept it from spreading.

"Not that one, not that one!" Ben decided.

The next rock I threw at the snake. Three snakes slithered into existence.

Ginger let out a terrified squeak.

"*Not* the snake," she said quickly.

With the fire still burning, and the snakes still sitting promptly upon their rune, I threw the last rock at the moon rune. Nothing happened.

"I still don't trust this, but that moon rune's the best chance we have," I told them. "Stay directly behind me."

I stepped on the first rune. I followed the path of the moon rune. My friends and I stepped on the same runes, walking in union. I reached out to grab the key. I had it in my hand, when the tile underneath us opened and we fell into darkness.

We let out ear piercing screams as we plummeted into the darkness below. I locked hands with my friends, Ginger on my right, Ben on the left. Jerry held Ben and Ginger's hands. We fell in a ring, until it broke becoming a fight of screams and flailing limbs.

"WE ARE ALL GOING TO DIE," Ginger screamed at the top of her lungs.

With the air rushing past my ears, I felt myself going lightheaded. When we hit the ground, I was expecting to land with a bone breaking thud, but it was surprisingly *soft.* I tried standing up, but my bones thought otherwise. Nothing was broken, which was good. We landed on a soft pile of *hay.*

"Wasn't expecting that," Ben muttered to himself.

I counted to 10 and tried to stand again. This time my leg bones seemed in favor of that idea and cooperated. I stood up, wobbling on my legs like a newborn horse.

"Everyone alright?" I asked brushing the hay off my clothes. Apparently, the words *are you alright* were my new favorite words.

"Besides having no idea where we are, not knowing where the exit is, or when we will

see light again, yeah I'd say we are doing pretty good," Jerry said sarcastically, standing up brushing hay off his clothes.

"Okay, okay, I get it we aren't at our prime, but we will figure this out", I told everyone, trying to muster a smile. But my lips wouldn't listen. I scanned my surroundings. We were standing on a pile of hay in the middle of a room. I looked down at my hand and I was still clutching the key.

It was small, about the size of my middle finger. It was shiny and bronze with a small sphere on one end, and opposite was the shaft of the key where you inserted it into the lock. This was it. How could something so small cause so much trouble? Something so small cost my friend's life. I wanted to throw the key away never to be seen again, but then the key would cause much more than a few lives to be lost. And my friend's lives could be included. So, I made a silent promise to myself that I wouldn't let Brooke's death be in vain.

I studied the room better. The room had solid marble floors, and quartz walls. There was a door behind me made of oak wood. And a double door in front of us, also made of oak wood.

"I vote we try the back door. It might lead outside," Ginger said.

I walked to the door, but it was locked. I tried to open it with the key, but it didn't work.

"Looks like we try the front door," I muttered.

I walked to the door with my friends trailing behind me. I lightly pushed on the door, and it creaked open. It opened into an elegant hallway. The same floors and walls were carried into the hall as the room we were just in. Portraits of the same man in different poses lined the walls. The man had dark brown hair and blue eyes. His features were sharp. His smile was there, but it was cruel. Just looking at the picture gave me the chills, and I could see it was affecting my friends the same way. I stared down the hall making sure it was clear.

"We have to be careful and quiet. I don't know where we are or who that is", I whispered, pointing to the portrait on the wall.

"I agree with Ariel," Ben said.

They followed me down the hall. I peeked around the corner and didn't see anything. We twisted and turned and got *nowhere.* Until we finally came to a pair of double doors.

There were two guards stationed outside the door. They wore black cloaks with a snake curling around a post on the sleeve. It was the same symbol that was on the tiles on the floor in the room with the key. The guards had their hoods pulled over their heads so we couldn't see their faces. They each had 3 throwing stars strapped to their left arm and an ebony sword strapped to the left side of their waists.

I pulled my friends back around the corner out of ear shot.

"I'm guessing we need to get in that room," I told them.

"As much as I want to disagree with that, I think she's right," Jerry said, sadly.

"How do we get past the guards?" Ginger asked curiously.

"A distraction?" Ben suggested.

"Maybe," I said

"Or tell them we are lost ..." Ginger said

"And risked getting killed? No way," Jerry said.

It turned into a quiet bickering until we decided that I should summon some rocks and turn us invisible. I threw the rocks, and the guards went to check it out and we creaked open the door. The same man from the portrait was sitting in the middle of the room in a chair with his back facing me and our friends.

"You can turn off your invisibility now," he told us. His voice was deep and rich. We didn't respond.

He turned and faced us, his sharp features and cruel smile didn't match his soft blue eyes.

"I won't bite," he promised. Though I had a feeling he might. I pulled out Brooke's
bag and safely stored the key in the bag. I nodded to my friends, and we stood tall revealing ourselves.

His lips twisted into a smile.

"Ariel Wends, I've been wondering when you'd show up "

"How do you know my name?" I asked, ignoring the way my eyes shifted to green out of fear.

"Do you know my name?" he asked with a smirk.

"No, should I?" I asked.

"Mhm, you wouldn't even notice your own uncle," he said. I felt my jaw drop.

He smirked. "Yes, Ariel, it is me. Uncle Shilo.

CHAPTER 12

I let out a gasp. How could I not recognize my own uncle?

"That's your uncle?" Jerry whispered in my ear, but I was too nervous to answer. And my eyes slowly shifted to Violet.

"I've been wondering about you being kaleidoscopic," he told me. I didn't know what to say.

"What is this place?" I asked him.

"This is one of the several bases of Taynam," he said. All the color drained from my face.

"Are you telling me... that you're Taynam?" I asked cautiously. He let out a laugh. A good hearty laugh.

"Of course, I'm not, I'll never be as great as him, but I try," he said. I couldn't believe my own uncle was working with the bad guys.

"I am one of the leaders of the Serpents, Lord Taynam's order. "

"Don't call him Lord!" I demanded. "He's horrible," I said with every bit of resentment I could muster. "He kidnapped *your* sister and my mother and if you're siding with him, you're just as terrible as Taynam himself."

"Wow, such confidence for somebody who's cowering behind her *friends.* Or are they your friends? Are they just using *you?* Do they make you risk *your* life for their personal

gain?" he asked me.

Each question weighed down on my shoulder. I could feel all the words burrowing into my head. I clutched my head trying to tune him out. I felt a hand on my shoulder.

"You're okay we'd *never* use you. We'd never do anything he just said we would." The voice sounded familiar. But, with all the words and thoughts spinning in my head, I couldn't place it. I focused on the words, but they sounded so faint. So close but so distant. Right there but far away. I calmed my breathing, refusing to play Shilo's mind games. I looked up and found my friends standing protectively around me.

"What did you do to her!" Ginger demanded

"I simply told her the truth," he said slyly.

"We would never!" Jerry yelled. "I already lost one friend and I refuse to lose another!"

I stood up, straightening my posture.

"It's ok," I told Jerry.

He whipped around to face me.

"How could you say that? It is not fine. We are lost and scared."

"Jerry, stop," I told him sternly.

He looked like he wanted to protest but Ginger pulled him back.

"What do you want?" I asked, my eyes shifted to a stormy grey.

"It's a simple bargain," he told me and my friends.

"And what is that bargain?" I demanded.

"You give me the key, and you and your friends leave with your lives." I laughed in his face, which confused him.

"Do you really want to kill your only niece?" Ben yelled at him. He didn't answer.

My confidence grew, returning my eye color to its normal hazel color.

"I have already been through so much. I've lost my friend. My friend almost lost his arm. I am Ariel Wends, and you can't scare me into submission. I'm no longer that scared girl running from the cops, afraid of what a new life would mean. I'm not that same person," I said. My eyes shifted into a bright yellow. A new color. Confidence." "You don't scare me," I said now in his face.

"But I do," He claimed.

"You used to. I will admit that. But now, now you are just another person in my way." My eyes glowed a bright, bright yellow.

"Your confidence is growing," he said, obviously seeing the change in my eye color. Me and my friends closed around him. Cornering him. Trapping him.

If he was kaleidoscopic his eyes would turn blue.

"Who's the one cowering now?" I asked.

He had no reply.

"I'll surely get punished for not bringing her back," he muttered under his breath. Shilo looked up at me and my friends. "You haven't seen the last of me," he claimed. I laughed in his face and slashed his arm. He grabbed hold of the wound trying to keep pressure on it. He let out a few half-hearted grunts.

"I'm sure this isn't the last time I'll see you," I told him.

"I'm doing this for *you,*" he promised. He snapped his fingers and disappeared.

"YOU'RE DOING THIS FOR ME?" I shouted to no one in particular.

I collapsed in a heap on the floor. With my head between my knees. For me? How could

he do this TO me? I knew he played mind games but not to this level. The sensible part of me knew he was lying. But the part of me that wasn't as sensible wanted to believe he was really doing this for *me.* That part of me wanted to believe so bad he was still him.

I was torn between two me's.

But deep down I knew the right thing to do. Let him go.

I was still deep in my consciousness, but something was off. Someone said my name.

Ariel, please wake up.

The voice got louder and took on a new tone of panic, desperately turning into a plea.

Please Ariel, wake up, you're - you're scaring me.

I tried pushing past all my fears to return to my consciousness. But I couldn't.

I just couldn't.

Ariel, Ariel.

The voice grew louder, and clearer.

I felt something cool press against my head.

I let out a muffled groan as the world around me became a bit clearer.

The white marble walls come into focus. Three people sat in a half moon around me. My eyes came into a full focus, and I could make out every detail around me.

That included Ben, with tears running down his cheeks. Jerry and Ginger had tears coming down their faces too.

"Don't you ever do that again," he scolded, waiting for me to nod before squishing me in a huge bear hug. Jerry and Ginger joined in piling up on top of me.

"What happened?" I asked.

"You collapsed on the floor and started rocking back and forth mumbling to yourself then you passed out," Ben said, and I noticed how puffy and red his eyes are.

"Don't think about that monster's mind games, he knew that was going to happen."

I tried standing up, which failed miserably. A few deep breaths later I tried to stand again and before I fell back to the floor Ben caught me and I leaned on him for support. I knew something was up when nobody teased me.

"What's wrong?" I asked shifting my weight from one leg to another.

They dismissed the question and I decided not to push it. After all they'd just been crying, thinking they had lost another friend.

"I know what will make you feel better," I said.

When nobody answered me, I said in my best Ginger impersonation, "Oh Ariel what's this idea? So glad you asked!"

I reached into Brooke's old bag and pulled out a tiny vile with a Murky gold liquid inside. I hobbled to the hay room and Ben struggled to keep up. I tried to open the back door.

And this time it opened. We were in a remote village somewhere along the south side of a long island. All my friends rushed outside and breathed in the fresh air. Then they saw I was still inside and plodded back to me.

"Go stand over there," I pointed to a tree 30 feet away. "And stay back."

They went and sat underneath the tree as I threw the gold bottle in the room and sealed the door. I ran as fast as I could to the tree and the room started to smoke.

"What did you put in there?" Jerry asked, then regretted asking when I replied with, "Explosives."

"Sounds like you," he said.

It was a ticking time bomb, but the vial finally exploded and sent the whole room up in flames.

CHAPTER 13

Almost as fast as we set the fire, we heard sirens blaring. Firefighters and paramedics rushed to the place of the fire. Thanks to the veil that protected Vetchers from human eyes we didn't have to hide our weapons. But we still rushed away unseen, so we weren't questioned or taken to the hospital. We went through an unnamed village and caught a bus to New York City. We still had to figure out the first puzzle that goes with the key. But who better to help with that than Calon, himself?

We arrived at the gates on a Monday morning. It appeared as if it was officially spring. The icy cold weather was gone, replaced by soft spring rains and damp air. The smell of fresh dirt and blooming flowers always helped with my queasiness. We walked up to the door and pushed it open. We saw a 5-year-old boy standing next to a six-year-old girl being lectured by Calon. The boy pointed to me and my group of friends and Calon turned to face us. His scrunched face turned into a huge grin.

"This is Ariel, Ben, Ginger, and Jerry," he said proudly.

"This is Leo," he said, pointing at the boy.

He had short-cropped coffee colored hair, bright green eyes, and a crazy smile. I glanced at the weapons my friends and I had, wondering if they could see them. Mr. C. saw the concern in my face and whispered, "Don't worry they are too young; they can't see it."

Then he pointed at the girl. "This is Sophie, Leo's sister." She had brunette shoulder length hair that contrasted with her glowing amber eyes. Her heart shaped lips curved into a smile when she saw us. Mr. C rushed them upstairs and took the four of us to his office.

Before I could stop myself, I said, "There was a girl named Brooke that lived here, right?"

He gave us a sad smile. "Yes, how did you know that? Did you meet her?" He sounded so hopeful, I almost wanted to dismiss the conversation.

"Yes," I said slowly. I took a deep breath and pulled the poppy flower out of my bag and set it on the table. He looked at me confused. I explained how we met her, what happened to her, and her secret base. We told him all about it.

He started to tear up and he looked at the poppy flower sadly.

"Oh," he said quietly when I finished. He took the poppy flower and set it promptly on his desk. Then I showed him the key and I explained everything we did on our trip.

Though I did leave out my conversation with Ben conversation because that wasn't mine to talk about.

When we finished, he looked at me and said, "I'm so sorry. I never knew it would be so brutal or I'd never have suggested you go." His voice cracked.

"No, it's ok. We needed to do this. I needed to do this. If I didn't, my parents would be dead by now. And honestly if you ask me, I think their parents may still be alive too," I said pointing to my friends.

"And I think you may be right," Calon said.

Even though we weren't sure I could feel the slight shift in the mood.

"We came to talk about the puzzle or test that we have to use the key for," I told him.

He looked confused." Isn't there a puzzle or something? It can't be as easy as collecting the three keys."

As if something that was out of place clicked in his head he said, "You're right. I will need to conduct a little bit of research, but I will inform you when I come up with something," he told us.

"That works," Jerry said.

"Woah, woah hold up everyone. How can we forget those cute little kids you were lecturing? Leo and Sophie?" Ginger asked.

Calon smiled. "They came to me earlier this week. I'd assume their parents, Mr. and Mrs. Johnson might be dead if it wasn't for you too," he said.

"Gee, no pressure there," Ben said under his breath.

I elbowed him in the ribs. "Ow," Ben yelped. Jerry and Ginger snickered, and when Ben glared at them, they just laughed louder.

"We will be doing everything in our power to help," I told Mr. Calon. He smiled. "I'm glad to hear that."

He dismissed us and we went upstairs to meet Leo and Sophie for real.

Ginger saw Sophie and immediately fell in love. And vice versa. Sophie loved Ginger. Ginger took Sophie out into the city. Jerry wasn't as smothering as Ginger, but he tried his best to talk with Leo.

With everything right in the world, I slipped out of the room and headed down the street to the public library. My first sort-of home. I thought I'd gone alone but walking along the streets I knew someone else was there. I unsheathed my dagger and turned around. Ben was standing there. I sheathed my dagger.

"We have had multiple conversations about not sneaking up on each other!" I told him.

He just smiled. I rolled my eyes. "You know you can't leave me there. It would have been awkward. A tween, a teen, and a five-year-old. Nuh-uh," he said.

"I'll give you that," I said, and we kept walking.

When we got to the library, I went around the back and climbed up to the roof. I took a deep breath and tried to relax. Being there made it feel much more *real*. Like finally accepting my life wouldn't be the same anymore.

"Is this where you used to live?" Ben asked me.

I nodded. "I think I might sleep here tonight," I told him.

"Why?" he asked.

"I don't know. It just feels … right. More like *home* than the orphanage."

"I get it," he said. "But what's the *real* reason you came here?" he asked.

He knew me too well. And I hated it. I knew him too well, and sometimes he probably hated it too, but I guess there was no reason to lie.

"I thought I could do some research on the keys. It's a legend so the library must have something on it," I said.

"Good idea, I'll help you look."

I was going to insist that he didn't need to, but if one of my friends wanted to help with something, they were going to help with it. I learned that the hard way.

We climbed down from the roof and walked into the library.

Ben scanned the Myths and Legends sections. Meanwhile I just asked the librarian.

"Ben, get over here," I whisper-hissed.

He came over to me and asked me what was wrong.

"We can just ask the librarian."

We walked up to the desk.

The girl sitting at the desk reading a book had a petite frame, light freckles, and her strawberry blonde hair was pulled back into a ponytail.

"Excuse me, miss," I said.

When the young lady looked up, she had light brown eyes flecked with bits of gold. Her pink lips in a smile as she said, "Ariel?"

"Amber?"

We jumped up and down and gave each other big hugs. Amber is my best friend, and she was devastated she wasn't going to see me anymore. She stepped back and studied me.

"You look so much...older, how old are you, twenty-six?" she asked jokingly I laughed.

"Only fourteen. But tomorrow I'll be fifteen. April 17th."

"Though I could say the same for you, are you 30 now?" I asked returning her earlier joke.

"Are you calling me old?" she asked with a laugh." No, I'm 15."

"Though, I did see you got yourself a boyfriend," she said happily.

Ben turned tomato red.

"He's not my boyfriend."

I had to be careful, making sure I didn't get embarrassed. I couldn't risk my eye color changing without knowing the veil would cover it.

"Riiiiiiight," she teased.

We aren't here to talk about this," I huffed. "Can you help us find any books about Taynam or the keys he's obsessed with?" I asked.

"Sure, but what's with the history and mythology? You hated that stuff."

"It's for.... a project at the orphanage. Ben and I are partners." And before she could tease about the partners part I added, "My friends Ginger and Jerry are helping too."

She gave us a section number and we went over to the aisle. We settled on two books. There was nothing useful until I found a passage about the keys.

The keys of earth core were Taynams main goal in life. He would kidnap children's guardians, forcing them to endure a quest to retrieve three keys. The next parts were

gibberish about things that weren't true. Until we came upon the section titled, KEY PUZZLES.

The keys each require a puzzle. The first puzzle for the bronze key is a simple symbol

etching. With a tool called a scalber, you must etch the following rune on the key's body.

It showed a symbol that was a star with a circle at each end. *If you have done it right and said the words mia milentia the key should glow a deep orange. If you have done it wrong however the key will turn a deep red and explode taking out any - and everything in a 10-mile radius.*

Then the passage ended. If everything this book was saying was true, I knew what we needed to do. I grabbed Ben's hand and moved to Amber.

"I'd like to check out this book," I told her.

I gave her my library card and stalked out of the library. I explained my plan on the way to Mr. Downs. And he completely agreed with my plan. We broke into a sprint and explained everything including my plan to everyone. We had to be vague with the plan, because of Leo and Sophie. And at their age they would think it's a game. A game that was way too dangerous.

We nodded in agreement, we agreed with the plan. After dinner and a nap, we headed back to Jericho. We needed to find Sam.

CHAPTER 14

We arrived the next morning. And I had no idea where to start looking. So, I did the first thing that came to my mind.

"SAM, SAM. GET OUT HERE I KNOW YOU HEAR ME."

And that he did. He still had the same dark brown hair, gray eyes, and pale skin. He dragged me and my friends into an alleyway.

"What are you doing here?" he said through gritted teeth.

"It's good to see you too!" I replied.

I pulled out the key and his face went blank.

"You got it," he said mesmerized.

I explained our theories and he surprisingly agreed.

"I'll put in a word with Leon for him to make a *scalber*," Sam said. Leon was the blacksmith that forged our weapons.

In the next hour we had a long eight-inch piece of obsidian with a sharp pointed tip. We took a bus to the place of our first Drython attack, deciding we wouldn't care if it blew up.

"Here goes nothing," I whispered to myself.

I touched the sharp edge of the scalber to the body of the key, carefully copying the rune from the book. I took my time, feeling the sweat pouring down my face. There were three options.

It didn't work.

It blew up half of Long Island.

It *worked.*

I was hoping for option number three.

I lifted the scalber and whispered the words the book told me. *Mia Milentia.*

For a very stressful second nothing happened. But the next second the key was glowing a deep orange. So far so good. The key lifted out of my hand as the etched star glowed a golden honey color. And then the key fell back into my hand. The star on it stayed that same color.

"Did it work?" Sam asked.

"I have no idea," I told him.

"Great," Sam muttered to himself.

I pulled out the book and read the next passage.

Based on the legend you know the etching has worked when it hasn't blown up. The etched star should remain the glowing gold color. If the golden color fades within five-minutes, then the key is no longer useful.

Well. That totally doesn't put pressure on the next five minutes.

And it's not like I could keep reading on the bronze key because then it went onto the silver key. The next five minutes were a ticking time bomb. But it was worth every second of it when the key stayed its golden color. I wanted to celebrate. But we couldn't. We had to get out of there and get to Plainview. But, of course, it wasn't so simple. I heard faint footsteps from the back of the clearing. The footsteps got louder and louder until a man was standing there with us. He started clapping slowly.

"Good job. You solved the puzzle. Got the key. So simple getting the others, right?" he taunted.

"You can already guess who I am," he said.

He was right. But I wanted him to be wrong so badly.

"Taynam," I whispered quietly.

"One point for Ariel!" Taynam cheered.

"What do you want?" I demanded. "Can't you at least hold off trying to kill us until we have all three of your keys? "

"I could. But I don't like to wait," he emphasized.

I let out a long sigh. Not only were we the ones trapped and cornered this time, but he was scary looking. Half of his face was scar tissue, and the normal half was scratched up. He had slick greasy black hair, and steel gray eyes. And he was wearing a black suit.... He was the man from my dream. I sucked in a sharp breath terrified, but I just kept thinking that we were the ones with no escape. What were we going to do? It seemed like *magic* was out. *Fighting* was out. And reason was definitely out. So, all we had left was to run. And he would most likely catch us. We could either fight a losing battle or … there wasn't really another option. I looked at my friends and we came upon a silent agreement. We couldn't *kill* Taynam, not without all three keys. But we could *weaken* him. Not for long. But long enough. I couldn't lose another friend. Not Sam. Not Ginger, Ben, or Jerry. So, I had to do this on my own. No help from my friends. I slowly walked over to my friends to show I posed no threat.

"Leave," I told them.

"Are you crazy? We aren't leaving you!" Jerry whispered.

"We aren't leaving you. End of discussion. I might not know you well, but we aren't going anywhere," Sam hissed.

Everyone nodded in agreement.

"Then you leave me no choice," I said. I didn't want to do it. But if they wouldn't leave, I'd have to make them…in a way.

I imagined myself putting a giant invisible dome around them. So, they couldn't leave, or fight. The force-field would die down if I died.

"I'm sorry," I said through tears. Most of their words were muffled but I could make out certain things.

Ariel, don't!

Please I can't lose you! We can Help!

I ignored them the best I could.

I faced Taynam.

"Let's get this over with, shall we?" I asked.

He didn't protest. I imagined the key in the force field with my friends and it popped into Sam's hand. That way Taynam couldn't pick it off me. I drew my dagger and Taynam drew his cavalry sword. The long steel blade had a perfect sharp edge. Its gold and leather handle fit perfectly in his hand. When my friends saw me draw my dagger and Taynam drew his sword, their muffled pleas for me to stop became more desperate.

"In the words of my own uncle, I am doing this for *you,*" I said to them.

"If I die, let them go. Take the key, or whatever but let them *go.*" I knew he'd still go after them, but I had to say it.

"Deal," he said. His lips curled into a smile, but the scar tissue side of his face just stayed still and motion-less

I gave one last look at my friends, since it could be the last time I saw them. But I didn't intend on dying. I took in a deep breath and charged Taynam.

CHAPTER 15

I got the first blow. I raked my dagger against his chest, ripping the fabric. He took a swing at me, but I ducked. He must be slow because I jabbed my dagger into his thigh, and he let out a yelp. I pulled it out and the wound was sticky with blood. He took a swing at me, and the blade grazed the edge of my arm. It was barely bleeding but it made me feel a little lightheaded. I used an invisibility spell to escape his next blow. I came up behind him, with my dagger above my head ready to strike. But before I could deliver, he spun around and knocked me to the floor

"Now, I know that old trick. I'm not a beginner, you know," Taynam chided.

"But do you know this one?" I asked, kicking him in the stomach to give me enough time to stand up. He grunted and said, "You never cease to surprise me, but I'm not so easily beaten."

He used Allusion magic to multiply himself, so now there were six Taynam's surrounding me. The real one somewhere among the fake. I focused all my mental energy feeling for body heat among them as they closed in around me. All of them radiated cold, except for one. I took out Brooke's old dagger from her bag. The handle still had dried blood

on it and it pained me to see it again, but I threw the dagger at the original Taynam. It caught him off guard and the dagger pierced his right shoulder. Taynam howled out in pain, and he yanked the dagger free. I hit an artery. Blood gushed out of the wound as he quickly applied pressure. But no matter how much fabric he ripped off his suit jacket the blood always seeped through. He gave me a glare as I could see him going weak. It looked like I'd won. But right before he snapped his fingers to leave, he threw Brooke's dagger back at me and it pierced through my left arm. I had just enough time to lower my friend's force field before the world went dark.

I regulated my breathing, so it was steady. And I was surprised to say, I wasn't in pain. And those words I hated.

That is what Brooke told me on her last breath. I opened my eyes and the world around me was a blur. I was still outside lying on the grass. I was glad I wasn't in a hospital.

Too many needles and stuff. And anyway, that would be hard to explain to a doctor.

So, you see my friend here was in a one-on-one battle with Taynam and she won but she was critically injured. Can you help her?

Yeah, nobody would believe that. I could hear Sam next to me muttering under his breath about how I was stupid, and honestly, I couldn't blame him. And this was all on my 15th birthday. Just how I love to spend my birthdays! When my eyes came back into focus, I could see Ginger sitting on the ground holding onto my right hand as Sam treated my left arm. Ben and Jerry were nowhere in sight. I didn't know if I could talk but I tried.

"Where are - Jerry-and Ben?" I coughed.

"They went to the store for painkillers and a *Surprise.* Though they wouldn't say what the surprise was," she said. "Now, rest."

Rest sounded good. But I couldn't sleep. "How long was I out?" I asked.

"One day."

I wanted to jump up and start moving. One day was one day too long. But I wasn't going anywhere. Just slightly shifting my shoulder felt like having a searing rod pressed through my forearm. I eased myself into a sitting position which took all my energy. I felt terrible. But I kept thinking happy thoughts. Meeting my father. Seeing my mother. Getting ice cream with my friends. Anything that would keep my thoughts away from the huge gash in my arm. It really didn't hurt. Unless I moved it.

Ben and Jerry returned. Ben came over and gave me a painkiller that numbed the area.

"We got something for you," he told me.

He walked over to me and handed me two boxes. One was brown and heavy. The other was small and wrapped in a light blue paper.

"Open the brown one first," Ben told me.

I did as he said. I opened the brown box first and a small cake sat proudly on the bottom of the box. It was a chocolate cake with blue vanilla frosting. On top written in loopy writing were the words *Happy Birthday Ariel.* I smiled.

"Thank you, guys!" I said.

Ben smiled and handed me the small light blue box.

"This is from all of us. They weren't with me, but Jerry and I both agreed everyone would think it's perfect," Ben said.

I pulled the paper off the box and opened it. Inside was a silver locket. It was small, about the size of a quarter. On the inside was a small picture of Me, Ben, Ginger, Brooke, and Jerry all standing in front of her flower bed. I forgot that day. We had just seen her hide-away and took that picture. I just hadn't realized it was printed out. It made me smile. Jewelry wasn't really my thing, but I could tell this is one thing I'd never take off.

"I love it," I told him.

"I knew you would," he said.

Ginger came around to me and swept my hair to the side to clasp the necklace around my neck.

"Let's eat some cake," I told them, attempting to stand up.

Ben grabbed one of my hands and Ginger grabbed my other hand and they hulled me to my feet. I wobbled over to the spot where we had a blanket set with the cake. When Sam didn't come over to us, I called over to him, "Get over here buddy, I might not know you well but unless you're allergic to chocolate or something you're going to *eat* some cake!"

He mumbled to himself and came over to us.

"You are just like having a little sister. Annoying, but I still listen to you," Sam said.

"That may be, *but* you know you like being my friend," I replied.

"When you're not almost dying, yeah!" I just rolled my eyes and we sat down.

"Before we eat, I just want to say, you will *not* be singing happy birthday to me."

They obeyed and I cut off 5 pieces of cake. We all sat in silence and ate our cake, but I couldn't stop looking down at my locket. It was such a thoughtful gift, and I love it but if I don't wear jewelry how'd they know I would like it? Maybe they just knew me better than I thought.

I barely finished half of my cake before I just couldn't eat anymore. Everyone else including Sam, Ben, and Jerry didn't finish their cake either. But Ginger, having a sweet tooth, finished all of hers and left no crumbs behind.

"I guess we should get going now. I want to show Sam the hide away," I said.

"Are you up for walking?" Sam asked. "We can wait another day."

"It's my arm that's injured, not my legs. I'll be fine for now," I told him.

"If you say so," he muttered.

We got onto the road, but I still had a slight limp. It was barely noticeable. *Barely.*

"Are you sure you're ok, Ariel?" Ginger asked, putting her arm around my shoulder so I could lean on her.

"Yeah," I replied.

We were almost to Plainview. Five more minutes. But I was pushing myself. My eyes turned a light shade of violet. Ginger stopped walking.

"Ok Ariel, seriously what's wrong? You wouldn't randomly be nervous," she said, studying

my eyes.

"I'm fine!" I snapped pulling away from her, so I was standing on my own. Three more minutes.

We could see the city. Two more minutes. I could make it to the hide away.

We were there. And being back just felt … wrong without Brooke.

I wasn't feeling up to it, but we went down to the bike shack and walked down the path.

After a while I veered us off the path and walked into the brush. Sam just stared blankly at the clearing.

"Wow this is some beautiful white fog," he said sarcastically.

"Sorry," I mumbled.

I walked over to him and put my hands on his temples. He flinched when I touched him.

I thought about how the camp looked and all the good memories, and granted him permission
to see it.

And when I took my fingers off his temples, for real he said, "Wow. This is actually really cool."

I went and sat down at one of the tables, while Jerry showed Sam around. Ginger went
and started digging around in the flower bed, planting new spring flowers. Ben came over and sat next to me.

"How's your arm?" he asked me.

"Numb, and sore at the same time," I replied. I just wanted to sleep but I knew I couldn't.

So instead, I took out my Journal and wrote about some of today's" accomplishments.

I could feel Ben looking over at my journal watching what I was writing. I closed up my journal and put it back into my burlap sack.

"Good night," I told Ben.

"It's five o clock," Ben replied.

"And all in one night I had a dagger go through my arm, *and* It was on my birthday. And you didn't do as much as I did, so I think I deserve a rest," I countered.

"I guess," he said and walked away.

I got my sleeping bag out and put it over by one of the lush trees. All the soft melodies of evening winds made my eyes heavy. The soft winds carried the cherry blossom petals through the air. The air smelled sweet. And without even noticing it I fell into a soft sleep.

CHAPTER 16

In the morning I awoke to a strange sound. It sounded like metal clanking on wood. I rubbed my eyes and slowly sat up.

"Look who's awake!" Ginger called, plodding over to me.

She had her hair styled in a messy bun, wearing a new light pink sweatshirt. I'm assuming her original one was torn up or stained with blood. She had on loose jeans and sneakers. Her eyes shimmered in the light, making her look older than thirteen. I just smiled at her.

"What time is it?" I asked her.

"Noon," she said.

"Noon?" I yelped and shot out of my sleeping bag.

"We figured you needed some rest, and it was best not to wake you," Ginger replied. I relaxed my shoulders.

"Well, I'm going to go get something besides my pjs on," I told her.

I walked up to the bathroom and got a familiar feeling. It was weird being back here. Where I first learned Allusion magic.

When I first learned I was kaleidoscopic.

The first place that even sort of, almost felt like home.

I slipped on a pair of black leggings and a camo tank top. I pulled my hair out of a ponytail and brushed it - which was a very painful process. When I got it all combed, I decided to leave it down. As much as I hate it, my mom was always telling me I looked better with my hair down. I walked out of the bathroom and joined my friends.

I turned to Sam.

"Are you going to stay here from now on? Or are you going to go back to Jericho?" I asked.

"I think I might stay here. Somebody needs to take care of this place. Or maybe I just want an excuse to stay." He smiled. That was the first time I'd seen Sam without all the worry on his face. He looked *happy.*

I smiled back. "I'm sure Brooke would approve."

I sat down underneath my tree. I wanted to stay here with Sam. I wanted me and all my friends to be safe, but I knew that wasn't the real reality I was facing. We still had to find two more keys, and we had no idea where to start looking. I just wanted a break, but that *break* could cost my family their lives. There was no telling how long Taynam was going to hold off before he came after us again. Jerry came over and kneeled next to me examining my bandaged arm.

"Is your arm feeling any better?" he asked, slicing the bandages off with his dagger.

"Yeah, it doesn't really hurt anymore. Thanks."

"No problem," he said.

The wound underneath was a deep scarlet red. Blood pooled around it.

"This part might sting a little."

A little was an understatement.

I had to bite my tongue when Jerry put a towel in the wound to keep myself from screaming. He cleaned the wound and sprayed it with a spray that stung like salt in an open wound.

I could feel bile coat my tongue as he took the towel away to show a raw, red wound. Good thing I didn't eat any lunch, because, if I did, I wouldn't be sure I could keep it down. Jerry finished wrapping the wound in a layer of gauze then a layer of white ace bandage.

He patted the wound and I had to fight hard to make sure I didn't wince.

"Thank you," I said.

"I told you, no problem. I'll always help one of my friends if they need it."

I nodded and Jerry walked away. I took out my dagger just to look at it. It had barely been a month and I'd already fought numerous battles with it. I gently traced my finger along the blade, being careful not to cut myself. I grabbed a rock off the ground and grazed the edge of my blade along it, attempting to sharpen it. Ben came over and sat next to me.

"How's your arm?

"Good."

"That's good."

There was an awkward silence.

Ben looked nervous, which made me nervous, and my eyes turned violet.

"Why are you nervous?" Ben asked

"I don't know, you look nervous, and it makes me nervous."

He gave me a sheepish grin. "Sorry," he said. "It's just that..." His voice trailed off.

"Do you trust me?" I asked him.

"Yes," he said without hesitation.

"Okay, then you can tell me what's on your mind. We can even go out of earshot from the others if you want."

He nodded and stood up and dragged me away from the others. We settled on the flower bed by the entrance.

"I've been thinking...probably more than I should be," he started off. "I have a question for *you*. And please answer honestly. "

I nodded.

"Do you think my parents are still *alive?*" I lingered on the question for a second.

"Yes. I think your parents are alive. If Taynam has eyes and ears all over the place he wouldn't kill them if he knew you didn't know about the keys," I concluded.

"How can you be sure?" he said, his voice almost not audible.

"I'm not sure," I admitted. "But no matter how evil he is, Taynam wouldn't kill them without a reason." I assured him. "I know that it's a hunch and normally my hunches are right."

He relaxed a little bit. Ever since we mentioned they could still be alive; he had been really tense. He got up off the ground and offered me a hand to get up. I accepted. "Thank you," he said. "...for everything."

"That's what friends are for."

He seemed a little caught on the word *friend,* he said Jerry and Ginger always viewed him a bit more as an older brother than a friend. And his only friend, Everly, had been brain washed so she thought he did something terrible that he hadn't.

I looked over at all my friends. We were finally a step closer to finding our parents. We were a step closer to ending this. We still have a long way to go, and good things don't last forever. But we can make the most of the good things while they are here. We still

have two more keys to find, and we don't know what challenges they will bring. But we *can* face them. My eyes shifted colors and turned bright yellow. Life will always throw you challenges (my challenges are specifically hard) and you must face them. But not *alone.* I took Ben's hand and strode over to my friends. This was one challenge we'd face together

The Key Chronicles

Silver

CHAPTER 1

"One more time!" Ginger commanded, though she was panting right along with us. We had already raced around the track field *ten* times.

"Can't we take a break?" Jerry whined.

My hair was plastered to my head with sweat, and all my limbs were starting to ache.

"Sorry Ginger, but I got to agree with Jerry on this one," I said, wiping the sweat from my forehead.

"Oh, come on! We are going to need to build up our endurance for fighting Taynam! Last time we were quick, but not quick enough," she complained.

I looked at the long white scar on my arm, from the time Taynam threw Brooke's dagger at me. Ben subconsciously looked at the spot on his arm a Drython had hit it. It didn't leave a scar, but the coloration is a slight bit darker there than the rest of his skin.

"I agree with Ginger that we need to be faster, but not that we need to run a bunch more laps around the field," I told the group.

Sam whined right along with Jerry. "Yeah, why do I have to train? I probably won't even go with you guys to get the next key."

"Better to be safe than sorry," Ginger countered. "But I guess we can take a break," she huffed.

"Thank you so much! You just saved my legs which threatened to fall off!" Sam said, giving her a big, sweaty hug. Ginger didn't seem to mind. We all headed back to Brooke's camp. But saying "Brooke's camp" all the time gets boring, so we decided to call it something else.

Sam thought we should call it "Camp Sam's Awesome," but we all decided against that. We had a lot of weird names for suggestions. Camp Awesomeness. Camp Cheese Doodles (that was Ben's idea). Camp Cocka-doodle-doo. And a few more. But ultimately, because I'm the best, we came upon the name I chose Camp Vetcher.

But really it just made sense. After all that's what we are called. And only the Vetcher's granted permission can see it.

When we got to camp Vetcher we took turns using the shower. Ginger insisted she went first since she said we could take a break, but Sam beat her to it. One hour later we all had on a fresh pair of clothes, and we were no longer sweaty. It was the middle of June, and it was 80 degrees outside. Ben had turned fifteen last month.

"Can we go get ice cream?" Ginger asked.

"Too much walking," Sam complained.

"You're impossible," Ginger told Sam.

"I know," Sam replied.

Ginger rolled her eyes and sighed. I went over and sat in the shade. Sam was in the

middle of constructing a house where the tent was. For the most part it was done, it just needed a few more tweaks. He said it would be better than sleeping in a tent every night. Though he did opt to keep the little shower room he had because then we could have two bathrooms.

It was a two-story house. The outside was a chocolate brown, and it had a porch with chairs and a small table. A black gable roof sat on top of the structure. There were five bedrooms, one for each of us. Plus, two guest bedrooms just in case. The bedrooms took up the entire second floor, considering they were each a master bedroom. On the bottom floor there was a good-sized kitchen nestled in the back left corner. They were ash wood countertops that sat ready on white cabinets. A dual stainless-steel sink was in the middle island. A double fridge was placed at the end on the counter running the side wall. A gas burner was placed parallel to the sink next to the fridge. We had a small wooden table with 6 dark oak cross-back chairs.

The living area was mostly downstairs. Two huge gray couches sat in front of a massive eighty-inch tv. A fluffy white rug was in front of the couches, and on top of the rug was a metal coffee table. Then there was the bathroom. It was just a simple glass shower, toilet, and sink.

We each got to design our own bedroom. My room had pale purple walls with

one dark purple accent wall. My queen-sized bed was pushed up against the dark purple wall. Each side of my bed had a small ash wood nightstand, with a lamp. There was a dresser at the foot of my bed. A chair and easel sat in one of the corners, canvas, pencils, paints, and paint brushes sat piled next to it on the floor. A gray rug in the middle of the room. Sam did a good job.

We were still outside complaining about the heat when I said, "Okay everybody! Calm down. Sam, I don't care how *tired* your feet are, we are going to get ice cream and that's that."

Sam groaned. "I thought you were on my side," he complained.

"I want ice cream, so we are going to get it." I told him.

He sighed, knowing I had made my mind up.

We got on the walking trail and headed out to Plainview. We stopped at one of the local Carvel's. The Woman at the counter had long black hair, delicate features, and bright sky-blue eyes.

"Hello! What would you like to order?" She asked. Her voice was soft and quiet.

I got salted caramel, Ginger got cotton candy, Ben got cookie dough, Jerry got pistachio, and Sam got plain chocolate. So basic of him.

"Forty dollars," she said with a smile. Sam handed her the money and she handed us our ice cream. We went and sat down at one of the tables. But I noticed something *off* about the cup it was in. Tied around the Styrofoam cup was a little note.

"Dear Ariel, Get here as soon as you can. I've got a lead.

- Mr. C."

Acknowledgements:

First and foremost, I'd like to thank *Megan Gillander*. She helped me a lot in this process. Megan is from the Oneida Public Library. She gave me suggestions on what to do and who to go to for help. It might have taken quite some time, but we finally got it done!

That leads me to thank the one and only renowned author and musician *Matt Pelicano*. He, along with Mrs. Megan were such a HUGE help. Matt did an amazing job, and an incredible amount of work to help me. He read an excerpt from my book and gave honest, trustworthy feedback. I worked off his suggestions and built my storyline more and did a bit of editing here and there. Finally, one of the parts that I will never forget was the fact he offered to proofread and do minor corrections. I will forever be grateful and will never forget their kindness.

My family and friends played a crucial role too. My dad and grandma, Nonie, did work to help too. Nonie read through a printed copy and hand-marked all the mistakes so my dad and his friend Meeghan McGahn could edit and fix them. They were very encouraging and supportive to me. My dad helped me through the all too long process of getting it published. He put in a lot of time and effort to make sure everything was perfect for me. It was worth it in the end. This was a long tedious process, but we got through it. Thank you so much. I Love you, dad!

My cousins were super kind and loved giving me interesting and funny asides to incorporate into the story. But the two I'd like to thank in particular would be Gracie and Aerielle. Gracie took all too much joy in making up weird characters. She definitely made things interesting. Aerielle was my inspiration for the name of the main character, 'Ariel'. She and my aunt couldn't wait for the book to come out. Hope you enjoy the book. Love you guys!

My mom, who I nicknamed 'Turtle', enjoyed my writing too. She and my stepfather were proud of me. I couldn't do this without their support too. Thank you for being there for me.

My other grandma also has a bit of a weird nickname, I call her 'Noodle'. Noodle ALWAYS wanted spoilers, but I'd refuse to tell her what the group's next adventure would be. She enjoyed reading it and providing me with her feedback. I have to say, it was funny watching her get stressed over some events that took place in the book. I love her so much and hope she enjoys the story.

Mrs. Harding, one of my first-grade teachers, and my favorite teacher by far said she love, love, LOVED this storyline. She always gave me encouragement, and when I had doubts she would always be there to tell me the story was awesome. She was proud of me, and I know that she truly enjoyed the story. Thanks so much.

Oh and Mrs. Harding, It's okay to lose! --Only she will know what that means.

Writing should be work, hard work, and that's true with a lot of crafts. If you truly love what you're doing, then you shouldn't be afraid to ask for help. You should want to improve your skills. I know I need a lot of help.

So, yet again I'd like to thank Matt Pelicano, Megan Gillander, Meeghan McGahn, Mom, Dad, Stepdad, Noodle, Nonie, Gracie, Aerielle, and Jennifer Harding. You all know what you helped me with, and I truly do appreciate all your love and support.